AF492759

An Event in Luxembourg

Howard Curtin IV

A3D Impressions

Tucson / Minneapolis

A3D Impressions™

Tucson / Minneapolis

An Event in Luxembourg
Howard Curtin IV

First A3D Impressions Edition August 2024

Publisher's Cataloging-in-Publication data

Names: Curtin, Howard IV, author.
Title: An event in Luxembourg / Howard Curtin IV.
Description: Tucson, AZ; Minneapolis, MN: A3D Impressions, An impression of
Awareness3D, LLC, 2024.
Identifiers: LCCN: 2024915356 | ISBN: 979-8-9890817-8-3
Subjects: LCSH Luxembourg--Fiction. | Europe—History--20th century--Fiction. |
Crime--Fiction. | Detective and mystery stories. | Historical fiction. | BASIC
FICTION / Mystery & Detective / General | FICTION / Crime
Classification: LCC PS3603 .U78 E84 2024 | DDC 813.6--dc23
LCCN 2024915356

Cover and book design: Donn Poll
Cover photo: Andrew Petrischev on Unsplash

This book is dedicated to
everyone who supported it
and made it possible. To Kate,
Donn and Rick, Mary Pat,
Mike, Howard III and Cathy,
and Hannah.

An Event in Luxembourg

ACT

I

Chapter 1
The Invitation

Cesar Mondragon had been to most of the major countries in Europe, but this would be his first trip to Luxembourg. It was a very small nation located between France, Belgium, and Germany, and had a population of no more than three-hundred thousand people. One would get the impression that it was a place where not much happened. It was therefore of little surprise to Cesar, that in his years as a private detective and inquiry agent, he had never been called to the tiny land of Luxembourg to address any issue that would merit the services of someone like him. It was therefore surprising to him, when three weeks ago he received a mailed invitation by one Alexander Decarli to join him and seven other guests for a formal gathering at the Hotel Geraldine in Luxembourg on the night of Thursday, August 3, 1939.

What had immediately caught Cesar's attention was the individual whose signature was on the invitation…Alexander Decarli. This was a name Cesar had heard before, during a case two years ago. The case had been innocuous at first, it was fugitive retrieval for the French police, which he had done for them before.

The fugitive in question was an unsavory sort named Antonin Rocca, a Corsican pimp who worked on the waterfront in Marseille (the French port city was the stronghold for the Unione Corse.) Even though his main business was prostitution, he was also knee deep in gambling and extortion. He would also kill someone for you if you offered him enough. Everyone knew who Rocca was and what he did, but the authorities had never been able to get their hands on him, because he was protected by powerful people. But this protection ended the moment he killed the wrong person.

Rocca had beaten to death a man he shouldn't have: A financier that worked on behalf of Parisian banking interests, a reputable man with powerful friends. Rocca either didn't know who he was killing, or he underestimated the consequences of such an action, but the result was the same: The people who had previously protected him were now content to hang him out to dry. The police were determined to knab Rocca and get him to implicate his criminal associates, those associates were just as determined to kill him to prevent such an outcome. He managed to evade both and fled to Italy.

A few weeks later, he was sighted in Venice. For some reason, the Italian authorities wouldn't cooperate with the French (even two years ago, relations between France and Italy had seen better days.) Cesar was hired to retrieve Rocca and bring him back to French soil. It took Cesar a few days, but he found Rocca in the Venetian district of Dorsodoro. He expected a fight when trying to apprehend the gangster and was surprised when Rocca agreed to go without a fuss. The only thing he requested in exchange was for Cesar to listen to him, because he had a story to tell him.

According to Rocca, he had been hired to kill the financier by a Swiss businessman named Alexander Decarli. Rocca had met him in a country inn late one night, only the bartender. Decarli was dressed in common clothes as he arranged the contract, eating seafood bisque and drinking rosé wine as if he had no cares in the world.

The financier was "inquiring where he shouldn't've been inquiring" regarding the business dealings of numerous prominent Marseilles residents, including members of the Unione Corse. Decarli played some part in those business dealings and needed the financier gone, and he needed it done by someone that couldn't be connected to him.

For that he needed a Marseilles waterfront cutthroat and Rocca matched this description. Decarli offered a considerable sum of money to blind him with greed, and he had said all the right things to alleviate any suspicions he had. Rocca was dismayed by how easy it had been to pull the wool over his eyes.

The day after he killed the financier, he was visited by a close associate that could be regarded as one of his few friends. The first words he said to him were "A Parisian was murdered in his hotel in the seventh arrondissement. Please tell me you had nothing to do with it." He spoke to a few more people after that, and it soon became clear to him how dire a situation he was now in.

He fled France before any of the knives came out and found some smugglers in Venice that agreed to shelter him. While in Venice, Rocca began to learn all that he could about Decarli and was able to use a contact the smugglers had in Switzerland to do so. He also had any loyal associates he had remaining in Marseilles inform the proper people that Alexander Decarli had requested and paid for the murder. Even if there was no saving himself, he was still determined to take Decarli down with him…But no one believed that Decarli had hired him.

Rocca learned from his contact in Switzerland that Alexander Decarli was an extremely secretive individual and hadn't been seen in several years. It was therefore glaringly out of character for him to have personally sought out Rocca for a murder contract. Decarli – in a moment of subtle brilliance – had done something that was so many leagues beneath him, that no one was credulous enough to believe he had done it. Rocca may as well have claimed that Prince Edward, Duke of Windsor hired him to kill the financier.

Cesar didn't know if any of this was true. It was quite a story and not something he believed Antonin was capable of fabricating. In the end though, Cesar didn't care, Antonin had committed many other crimes that he was guilty of, and Cesar had been hired to bring him to the French police. In the end, that was what he did.

A few months later, he heard from one of his sources that Rocca had died in a Marseilles prison in an apparent suicide. This made him curious enough to track down Rocca's contact in Switzerland, but he was unable to do so as the contact had disappeared. He also found some of the smugglers in Venice, the ones who Rocca had mentioned by name. Not only did they have no information to give him, but they rather forcefully denied having met Antonin Rocca or even knowing who he was. From that point on, Cesar promised himself that he would not forget the name Alexander Decarli.

Two years went by without Cesar hearing so much as a mention of the name Alexander Decarli, but now he had received an invitation to a Luxembourg hotel with the man's name on it. The next thing he noticed was the names of the other people on it, including his own name. There was a list of eight people who would be attending as guests of the party. Felix von Strichtenheimer of Austria, Dieudonne Galopin of France, Sergei Melikov of Russia, Kenneth Pryce of the United Kingdom, Pietro Biassiano of Italy, Ludwig Rombauer of Germany, Francis Edmund Dickerson of the United States, and Cesar Mondragon of Mexico.

Cesar hadn't ever received an invitation to a formal party, but he did not believe it was customary to list the names and nationalities of the other guests on invitations. This was curious to Cesar for two reasons. The first was that all the guests were of a different nationality, Cesar as the eighth guest was Mexican. Decarli the host was Swiss, which meant that members of at least nine nationalities would be at the Hotel Geraldine on August 3, and they would all be men. He wondered what, if any, significance there was to this, and if it was by design.

The second curiosity was that if Decarli did indeed send these invitations, it would mean he knew that Cesar was from Mexico. Considering that Cesar Mondragon wasn't even his original name, and that he had been using a series of aliases ever since he left Mexico in 1920. This either meant that the person who sent the invitation had speculated somehow of his origins in Mexico, or that they were aware of his true identity. He believed the latter was likelier, and that was a matter of concern to him.

Eventually after rereading the invitation three or four times, Cesar began to deliberate upon a course of action. The most evident action would be to follow through with the invitation and arrive at the Hotel Geraldine on the night of August 3. However, this was, in all likelihood, what was expected of him from the person who sent the invitation, and he knew that there was degree of risk in being predictable and compliant.

Another course of action would be to not follow through with the instructions of the invitation and to instead conduct his own investigation regarding the person or persons who had sent this invitation. The first objective of such a course of action would be to locate Alexander Decarli and ascertain if he was actually the one who sent the invitation to Cesar. If Decarli had in fact sent the invitation, then Cesar would demand answers from him. But if it turned out that someone had sent the information using Decarli's name, then Cesar would be confronted with a much stranger ordeal.

It was also worth looking into the other seven guests. Had they received similar invitations as well? Because if Cesar's invitation was the only one of its kind, then that would indicate that this was somehow about him. Locating Decarli would be difficult enough as it was, doing the same for seven other people would be an excessively laborious task.

Whether or not he would accept the request of the invitation and attending any alleged function at the Hotel Geraldine, he was determined to know more about Alexander Decarli and the other seven people. And for that, he required the assistance of others, which fortunately was precisely what he had.

Cesar was acquainted with many people in Britain and mainland Europe that had proven to be reliable and resourceful sources of information to him. When he needed details about a person or subject of interest, he enlisted their help. Some of them did it as a favor to him, others did it for payment. He was content with either so long as they produced what he needed.

Obtaining information about eight men though would prove a significant task, a task that only one of his contacts was suitable for: Philip Abendroth was a fellow private investigator that Cesar had known for roughly five years. He'd been active on the continent for far longer than Cesar and had a network of information gatherers that stretched as far as Turkey.

It took Abendroth two weeks, and cost Cesar a sum of money he'd been sitting on, but it was a successful endeavor. When Abendroth reconvened with him, he was pleased to say that enough information had been obtained to produce a profile of the seven others on the guest list and Alexander Decarli himself. All eight dossiers we're left in Cesar's dead drop in Cutteslowe.

Francis Edmund Dickerson was born in 1885 to a family that would make their fortune during the Arizona copper boom. His childhood was spent in both Bisbee and his native Ohio. He attended prep school and Northwestern University before taking an official position at his father's company. In the time since then, he's worked as a treasurer for numerous American companies as well as philanthropic societies. Even though Dickerson belonged to America's Republican Party, he was in excellent order with FDR and the New Dealers. He has also recently begun to make appearances in British and French social circles.

Kenneth Pryce was born in 1899 and would be turning forty later that year. He was born into a middle-class family in Gloucestershire. He was conscious of class differences from a young age and would become politically sapient by the time he was a teenager, identifying as a socialist at sixteen. He attended the University of Bristol; but was forced to leave during his third year after he was revealed to belong to a student group opposed to British activities in Ireland. He went on to become a journalist and photographer and has had his work featured in many left-wing publications. Pryce was a vagabond and never seemed to stay in one place for long. He hadn't been back to his home country of England in years and was none too popular with the authorities there.

Dieudonne Galopin was born in 1887 and was part of a family legacy of French soldiers and sailors that dated all the way back to the French Revolution. When the Great War first broke out, he was a young Lieutenant in the French Army. By the end of the war, he was a Captain who had gained a reputation for his critical attacks of France's military bureaucracy and their disregard for the lives of their own soldiers. He was present for the French Army mutinies of 1917 and played a committed role in resolving them peaceably. In 1926, the French Ministry of War gave him a desk job where he's remained ever since. During the Spanish Civil War, he was an outspoken advocate of the Republican forces and repeatedly called on the French government to do more to help then. Ever since the war ended with a Nationalist victory in April, he has had suspiciously little to say about the topic.

Dr. Ludwig Rombauer was born in 1878 to a Bavarian father and a Rhinelander mother. He was a prodigy who had completed his conventional schooling at age fifteen and attended prestigious institutions such as the Technical College of Berlin and the Prussian Academy of Sciences. When he was still in his twenties, he was recruited by the German government to work as an engineer on weapons development for Germany's military. He was said to have played an unseen role in several of Germany's technological breakthroughs and had good relationships with many arms manufacturers, the Krupp family chief among them. He left Germany soon after the country's defeat in the Great War, and had since then taken up residency in Gothenberg, Sweden, where his continued engineering work has been patronized by the Swedish government. With war once again looming in Europe, his native Germany (now under Nazi rule) has tried to persuade him to return to weapons development, but he has proven to be unreceptive and evasive.

Felix von Strichtenheimer was the youngest man there, born in 1905 as the third son of an Austrian noble family. The family was the subject of a scandal in the years leading up to the Great War, but it was something of a taboo subject and most weren't clear on what occurred. Much of the official information about the scandal "disappeared" during the tumult of the war and Austria-Hungary's dissolution. What was known was that Von Strichtenheimer's two elder brothers died fighting in the war. When the Habsburg Law was passed in 1919, he along with the rest of the Austrian nobility lost their titles and privileges. His family left Austria soon after and took up residency in the Netherlands. He attended school in England, studying at New College, Oxford. He lived somewhere in the Dutch city of Eindhoven, subsisting off the inheritance that was meant for his dead brothers and the proceeds of a book he had written at Oxford. He valued his privacy.

Sergei Simeonovich Melikov was born in 1894 to parents that belonged to the merchant class of Imperial Russia. He attended the University of St. Petersburg where he studied history and mathematics. After finishing his schooling, he worked for a short time in a bank, but lost his job after the bank was robbed and burned down during the February Revolution of 1917. He then found work as a low-level clerk in Alexander Kerensky's government. However, the October Revolution would bring the Bolsheviks to power, and he fled the country along with hundreds of thousands of other Russian nationals. For the past twenty years, he has been living in Copenhagen and working as an accountant.

Pietro Biassiano was perhaps the most notorious of all the guests. He was born in 1892 in the Northern Italian region of Emilia-Romagna and studied philosophy and political sciences at various colleges in Bologna. When the Great War began, he interrupted his schooling to join the Italian army. He was decorated for his actions at the Battles of the Piave River and Vittorio Veneto and left the war as a commissioned officer. Soon after the war, he went to Rome to study law and became an enthusiastic follower of Benito Mussolini. He joined the National Fascist Party in 1921 and the Blackshirts in 1923 and was one of 30,000 militants to participate in the March on Rome that brought Mussolini to power. In 1924, he became Italy's youngest prefect at the age of thirty-two and was put in charge of eradicating the Mafia in a particular province of Sicily. In the years since then, he has been responsible for the deaths of nearly thirty people, the majority of whom were alleged Mafia members.

And then there was Alexander Decarli, the host who had invited the other seven. When Cesar opened his dossier, he found that Abendroth had left him a note, which he hadn't done for anyone else.

Out of the eight names you gave me, Decarli was the most difficult to ascertain information about and represents the largest part of your debt to me. I had to contact an individual that I don't contact for no reason and make a promise to another individual who I'm apprehensive of. But because of my efforts, you know now more about Alexander Decarli than anyone else on your side of the English Channel.

Decarli was born in 1883 north of the Swiss-Italian border. There were many apocryphal theories about his lineage, with assertions that he was a descendant of one or more of history's most powerful families: The Capetians, the Medici, and even the Julio-Claudians. What was known for sure was that both his parents came from old Swiss families.

Alexander had an older brother and younger sister, but it was an unspoken truth that he was the most talented of them, as although he was shy and quiet, he was very intelligent and displayed talent in humanities, natural sciences, and chess. When he was ten, his father became estranged from his mother and went to the Campania region in Italy to work as an animal breeder. When not in Switzerland with their mother and sister, Alexander and his older brother would travel by train to Italy to live with their father.

It is unknown exactly how or when, but while in Campania, Alexander and his brother became involved with the Camorra, a crime syndicate that was native to the region and had a far fiercer reputation than the Mafia in Sicily. The Decarli brothers were originally low-level associates of the Camorra who engaged in petty thievery, but due to Alexander's intelligence and organizational skill, they soon become the leaders of their own major extortion ring. However, the Camorra would soon appropriate the extortion ring for themselves, and Alexander and his brother would return to Switzerland for good.

Alexander did not attend a university and instead became the apprentice of the wealthy owner of a watch company. He would spend the next ten years of his life learning the lessons of commerce and finance. Upon the death of the owner of the watch company, Alexander would inherit the estate as the owner and his wife were childless. In just a few years' time, he expanded the watch company into a multi-faceted enterprise that had holdings in every sector of the Swiss economy.

Decarli was very flamboyant with his newfound wealth and enjoyed a bachelor's lifestyle. He was known for the parties he held every Summer and Winter at his castle estate in the Swiss Alps. The guest lists for the parties were quantifiably grand and included people from all corners of Europe. Some even came from as far off as the Americas or Asia, crossing the Atlantic or even a continent just to take part in the glamor of one of Decarli's grand events. People who attended the parties would come back with stories of how "raucous" and "ill-mannered" they were. This naturally led to some of the more conservative and prideful members of elite society to shun Decarli and his invites out of principle.

Naturally, Decarli's parties also became something of a haven for outcasts and eccentrics. He would embrace this, inviting those that were accused of homosexuality and other taboos, those who had been involved in scandalous affairs and we're now ostracized. In aristocratic families and high-end social circles, the phrase "exiled to the Swiss alps" was commonly used to indicate someone who was persona non grata. Another was "even Decarli wouldn't have you/them." He also invited underclass individuals if he enjoyed them enough: A man who cleaned the floors of a bank in Zurich, people who worked in one of his favorite restaurants, a destitute man who he had encountered on the street and struck up a conversation with.

Despite never marrying or settling down, he did eventually produce a daughter. Born in 1912, her name was Valencia, and the identity of her mother was uncertain to the point of it being not worthwhile to make assumptions on the matter. After she was born, the parties happened less and less, and when they did, it was usually because she was somewhere else. But she was more often than not in the company of her father, who delighted in taking his daughter and her au pair along with him on his travels. When she reached a certain age, she would sit near him or even on his lap during important meetings he had. He would disregard suggestions that she leave the room and explained that she was good enough to learn and understand everything he did. On the occasions where he was asked if he would like a male heir, Decarli would respond "Valencia is all I need."

The beginning of the Great War and all the events that came with it would provide Decarli many more opportunities for expanding his power, wealth, and influence. With much of Europe destabilized from the war, Switzerland became a haven for foreign capital and experienced a growth in its banking industry. Decarli was one of many Swiss businessmen that shepherded the growth of the banks and even started some of his own. As a banker, he was known to do business with anyone and everyone regardless of who they were or their affiliations. He had connections to every major crime syndicate in Europe, not just the Unione Corse and the Italian syndicates, but the syndicates of Britain, the Penose in the Netherlands, and the Ringvereine in Germany. In the aftermath of the Russian Revolution, he would aid exiled Russian aristocrats by providing them with underground vaults to lock up their riches in, and at the same time helped Bolshevik-aligned individuals hide items that had been looted during the Revolution. He was also allegedly involved with both sides of the conflict in Ireland, but what that involvement was varied depending on the source of the information.

This gained him a reputation as an unscrupulous opportunist with no loyalty to anyone. The one man in Switzerland who best exemplified the national policy of neutrality. The man who would shake the hand of both you and your worst enemy and then whisper to each of you that "we're playing him for a fool, aren't we?" The man who would sell you the rope to hang yourself with, and if the rope were to break would tell you he sold you a weak rope to save your life.

Decarli naturally saw it in more flattering terms, once telling a colleague "I don't believe I'm suited to pass judgments or be sanctimonious about who I engage with and believe that impartiality and professionalism are the greatest traits I can have as a businessman." He said this the same way he had said everything else, with such a graceful and deliberate use of the spoken word that it was difficult to discern whether it was genuine.

His most profitable venture was the dealings he had with American financial interests that funded the reconstruction of Europe after the war ended. By the end of the 1920s, Decarli was among the wealthiest men in Switzerland, and while he was by no means a celebrity in Europe, his name was whispered in the circles of politics, finance, and crime. If one knew he was, then they knew why he mattered.

The Global Great Depression would cost Decarli a fraction of his fortune, but still left him very wealthy. He consolidated what was left of his assets and disappeared from the public eye, the only people routinely in contact with him would be his closest advisors and his daughter Valencia. Throughout the years since then, Decarli would involve himself with some affair or enterprise, as if to prove to himself and everyone familiar with him that he was still a palpable presence in the order of things. Whether it be making investments in armaments, influencing Swiss banking policy, or plotting with the Unione Corse, Alexander Decarli would consistently affirm that he was an unseen power, not unlike a ghost or a god.

Cesar stayed up late at night reviewing the information he had compiled on Decarli and the seven guests. This was a most unusual assortment of characters, Cesar had met many unique and interesting people in his years, but never had so many of them been in one place at one time. Decarli, the one who sought to gather them together, was the most unique and interesting of them all.

At a certain point during his accumulation of information on Alexander Decarli, Cesar underwent the realization of how unfeasible a course of action it would be for him to locate and confront the Swiss millionaire on terms that were favorable to himself. Decarli was someone of grand initiative and scope. Cesar, as a private investigator who made his livelihood working for police services and well-off clients, was rather less impressive. Making Decarli his opponent without any indication that it was unavoidable or necessary would be an act of foolishness.

Therefore, Cesar concluded that the best possible course of action was to follow through with the invitation and join Decarli and the other guests at the Hotel Geraldine at the time and date of the invitation.

Would such harm come to Cesar simply by accepting the invitation? Decarli was not a lowly highwayman who sought the wealth of a passing carriage, nor was he a malevolent madman that maimed and murdered everyone he came across. Decarli was a sophisticated specimen, and his intention for this formal gathering of eight specific guests would unquestionably be an issue of intrigue. Cesar would want to know more about that issue of intrigue, and it was for this reason above all others that he would be attending this formal gathering in Luxembourg.

With his course of action clear, Cesar ensured that any affairs he had were in order, packed a single case that consisted of his clothes, a proper amount of spending money, travel papers, a journal, three pencils, and his LeMat Revolver; and proceeded to craft his travel plans. On the day he was to depart from his home in Oxford he ate breakfast and hurried out the door. In the forty-one years of his life, Cesar Mondragon never once chose a course of action that was passive or indecisive, he would directly confront every situation he came across with both serious conviction and an awareness of his limitations. It had served him well and he believed it was the reason he was still alive after all this time. He would have to trust that it would serve him again in as he met whatever awaited him at the Hotel Geraldine.

Chapter 2
The Hotel Geraldine

To get to his destination, Cesar boarded two trains and one ship. The first train was from Oxford to the Southern Coast of England, from there he boarded a ship that crossed the English Channel to France, the last train took him to the France-Luxembourg border. Gaining entrance to France and Luxembourg proved to be an obstacle as in both instances the customs officers were problematic. In the last few years, Cesar had noticed that traveling between the various countries of Europe had become more cumbersome, which was understandable given the present political climate in Europe. Fortunately, he was more familiar than most with the process of navigating international borders and carried the proper documents and finances.

Once in Luxembourg, he procured a 1938 Mercedes-Benz and a road map of Luxembourg from a German car rental service. Even though it was a very small country, it was still big enough to be divided into two regions. Luxembourg's main region was "Gutland" and covered the southern part of the country, it was the more urbanized part of Luxembourg and therefore where the majority of the population lived. Gutland was the part of Luxembourg that Cesar had arrived in.

The north was "Oesling" and was the more rural part of Luxembourg, it was known for its hills and had a much smaller population that lived in various small villages that were far apart from one another. The Hotel Geraldine was in Oesling. While at the car rental service, he inquired about the hotel's location and a helpful woman had marked it on his map with a X. Cesar thought it was unusual to mark the hotel's location with X, but he remembered how small a country this was and thought it appropriate.

Since there was still a day before the gathering at the Hotel Geraldine and it would not take very long to travel there, Cesar spent the night and the next morning at an inn in Gutland. The next day he had a valet retrieve his Mercedes and he began his trip across Luxembourg. He marveled at what a pristine place Gutland was with its beautiful buildings and bustling communities, but when he entered the Oesling, he had the unmistakable feeling of coming home after a long journey.

Oesling was a pastoral place, not unlike where Cesar spent his younger years. There was a strong sense of what could be, or what already was but had yet to be discovered. All around there was wilderness, and where there was wilderness there was the unknown, and all the implications that the unknown carried. Sporadically through his drive, Cesar would spot a stone castle in the distance. These castles served as a sobering reminder to him that as with all pastoral settings human intrigue was still present, not present to such a magnified degree as with cities, but present nonetheless.

Cesar arrived at a turnoff from the main road, near the turnoff was a sign with an arrow that read "Hotel." He didn't know how many hotels were in the area marked on his map, but he was fairly certain that the "Hotel" proclaimed on the sign was the Hotel Geraldine. He turned off the road and drove through the wilderness. The road ended at a pair of gates that were open, another nearby sign announced his arrival at the "Hotel Geraldine." As he drove past the gates, he finally received a look of the hotel.

He was by no measure an architect or an authority on European buildings, but from what Cesar could see, the Hotel Geraldine appeared to be a very old structure originally built during the Late Medieval Period or the Renaissance, although various aspects of its appearance indicated that it had been restored to a good state of repair in the recent past. The color of the walls was far too light for such an old building and the roof had been painted black recently. One of the chimneys was starkly different from the others, its bricks were newer, which indicated that there had been an old chimney that had been replaced. Aside from these observations, Cesar saw that the Hotel Geraldine was three stories tall and that the surrounding landscape and trees were remarkably well cared for.

He noticed a long row of cars parked in front of the hotel and parked the Mercedes next to them. He exited his car with his case, but did not immediately enter the hotel, he instead took a minute to survey his surroundings and listen to what his intuition told him about the new place he was in. When his intuition revealed nothing of interest, he took note of the setting sun and entered through the hotel's front doors.

The lobby was not as large as Cesar thought it would be. Additionally, it was darkly lit which he thought was peculiar. The walls were painted green and the floors were grayish-blue marble. Across the lobby was the front desk, and on either side of the desk was a stair case. To the side of the lobby was a lounge area where there was an assortment of furniture and tables. Two arched entryways led to other areas of the ground floor.

The only two people in the lobby aside from him were a woman reading in the lounge area and the concierge at the front desk. Cesar walked up to the front desk. Even though the concierge was able to see him approaching, he looked pointedly away until Cesar was standing in front of him, and then regarded him with interest.

"I am expected here" Cesar said plainly.

"And you would be?"

"My name is Cesar Mondragon."

The concierge stared at him for a few seconds before turning his head in the direction of the lounge area where the woman was. Cesar looked towards the lounge area, and was about to turn back to the concierge, when he noticed the woman rising from her seat and striding purposefully over in his direction.

The woman walked in such a way that one received the impression that she held unseen power and authority. She had curly reddish-blonde hair and light blue eyes. She was dressed casually conservative in a green blouse, a dark blue skirt that went all the way down to her ankles, and dark brown boots that were barely visible under her long skirt.

As she came closer, Cesar noticed that her skirt wasn't a conventional skirt, but rather a split skirt, otherwise known as culottes. They were wide-legged pants that had once been formal wear for men, but during the Victorian era had become popular with woman for use in horseback-riding.

"Mister Mondragon" she declared, making his name sound regal. "I would welcome you, but I have always detested the word 'welcome.' I believe it to be an insincere word you see. I will instead affirm that you are indeed expected, and trust that this is sufficiently ingratiating for a man such as yourself?"

Cesar was rather stunned, not just by the words 'sufficiently ingratiating,' or the notion that the word 'welcome' could be insincere, but by the energy and confidence in the woman's voice. She spoke to him, a person she never met, with such insistency and assuredness that Cesar was inclined to recollect if he had met her before. However, he could make no such recollection, and felt himself obligated to inquire.

"I don't believe you and I are acquainted."

"Are you not acquainted with Mister Decarli?" she asked patiently.

He was unsure of how to respond "I...I cannot claim to have met him."

"Have you received an invitation from Mister Decarli?" she asked just as patiently.

"I believe that I have yes, if you would like to see it…"

"That won't be necessary. Nobody here will insinuate that you're not Cesar Mondragon, or that you did not receive an invitation."

She said this all very quickly. Cesar studied the woman, not knowing what to make of her. She simply observed him with a courteous expression. It eventually occurred to Cesar that she was waiting for him to make the next remark.

"I see."

She nodded contently and looked at the concierge, who placed a key to a room on the desk in front of Cesar.

"If I may, Mister Decarli wishes me to accompany you to your room and then take you to join the others. You are the last guest to arrive and we are eager to begin."

"Begin what?" Cesar asked quickly.

She looked at him strangely and then quickly moved in the direction of the stairs. He looked towards the concierge once more and saw that he had returned to looking away as if Cesar wasn't there. Not knowing what else to do, he grabbed his room key and followed the unknown woman as she ascended one of the staircases.

The woman led Cesar to his room on the second floor, it was an attractive four-poster bedroom with colors of purple and white. The paintings that were in the room caught Cesar's attention, he saw that they were nailed to the wall.

Cesar used to live in the United States, and for some reason, many American hotels nailed their artwork to the walls so it couldn't be removed. When he came to Europe, he learned that European hotels didn't seem to have this practice…The Hotel Geraldine was the first exception he encountered.

Cesar had a premonition that a miniscule fraction of his time at the hotel would be spent resting in his room. As if to legitimate this premonition, the woman only provided Cesar with a few minutes to change into fresh clothes and then politely asked him to follow her to the hotel's drawing room.

The drawing room was on the first floor and was located somewhere in the internal workings of the Hotel Geraldine, Cesar had followed the woman through several of the second-floor corridors and then down a discreet spiral staircase that had the deceptive appearance of being servants' stairs. At the bottom of the spiral stairs was the drawing room, which had no windows and two closed doors.

Assembled near the drawing room's fire place were the seven other guests, who Cesar observed were sitting far away from each other and did not appear to be enjoying each other's company. They were partaking in coffee and brandy, which gave a few of them an excuse to not engage with each other.

The woman led Cesar to these "Gentlemen, I introduce you to our final guest, Cesar Mondragon."

She introduced each man to Cesar, which gave him the opportunity to observe them all.

Francis Edmund Dickerson sat confidently in his chair and gestured towards Cesar with his brandy. He had grayish-black hair, hazel eyes hidden behind rectangular glasses, and a prominent mustache. He was a tall man that eradiated power, but it was a power that was more paternal than outright malevolent or tyrannical. Cesar briefly thought of Teddy Roosevelt in his older years.

Kenneth Pryce had been taking care of himself and did not look a man who would soon be forty. He had blue eyes, light brown hair, and the face of a choir boy. He looked at Cesar curiously, smiled at him, but then looked away. Cesar could tell that he was vulnerable and defensive, he sat on the edge of his seat with arms in front of him.

Dieudonne Galopin drank his brandy with unceremonious zeal and slouched in his seat, suggesting a lower-class background that he remained loyal to. He was tall like Dickerson but was much more broadly built. He had black hair in a soldier's cut, grayish-blue eyes, and a square jaw. He stared hard at Cesar as if suspicious of him. The way he carried himself reminded Cesar of a tired horse or bull that had been overworked and wanted nothing more than to rest.

Dr. Ludwig Rombauer was easy to spot as he was the oldest guest there. He didn't quite have the appearance of a distinguished engineer, sporting a rather grandfatherly and gullible smile as he said "Hello" to Cesar. He was a short and rotund man with balding gray hair and a goatee.

Felix von Strichtenheimer had the appearance of an intense young man. Even though he was in his thirties, he could pass for a college student. He had well-groomed brown hair and his solid brown eyes stared energetically at Cesar. His face was sharp, serious, and sad, yet also proud.

Sergei Melikov was a very placid looking person and gave very few hints as to what his personality was like. He had prominent lips, well-groomed black hair, and green eyes behind a pair of gold-rimmed glasses. He looked at Cesar with complete neutrality.

Pietro Biassiano was undoubtedly an aggressive person just by the way he sat in his chair. He was perched on his seat like a bird, as if at any moment he would be expected to leap to his feet and perform some deed of righteous action or violence. He had reddish-blonde hair and hazel lion-like eyes. He did not seem interested in looking at Cesar.

"As you can see, we've saved a seat for you." The woman gestured to Cesar to an empty chair between Biassiano and Rombauer. As he sat next to Biassiano, the Italian Fascist looked at him for the first time. Cesar made the effort not to look at him and instead looked towards Rombauer, the German engineer seemed relieved to have someone between him and Biassiano. The woman walked in front of a fireplace that was near them and turned to address the group of eight men.

"For those of you who are unaware of who I am. My name is Valencia Decarli."

Cesar had not been able to observe the reactions of the others as he was so surprised himself. He looked at the woman who had greeted him as if seeing her for the first time. This was his daughter, who he valued over the prospect of a first-born son and one of the few people who truly knew him.

"It is a pleasure meeting you" Dickerson said, the first guest to speak.

"The pleasure is all mine, Mister Dickerson. Regrettably, it is not me that you come all this way to see. You are guests of my father Alexander, he is not merely the one who invited you all here, but the one individual that you are all acquainted with."

"I...don't believe I am acquainted with him" Dickerson said.

There was a murmuring of concurrence.

Valencia gave them all a look that Cesar couldn't help but think was condescending. "Even though there are those among you who're not familiar with him, he is familiar with you. For each of you here, there is an issue of importance that he desires to speak to you about. Given that each of you live in different locations across Europe, he thought it more prudent that you all enjoy one night's worth of his hospitality at the Geraldine. By inviting you here, he will be able to converse with each man about the issue of importance, and within the course of one night's event."

Kenneth Pryce tired of staring at his hands and looked at Valencia. "This formal gathering as you call it, it's not simply an exercise in bourgeois sentimentalism? There is actually a reason for each of us to be here?"

A few of the men in the room stared at Pryce for his use of the expression 'Bourgeois sentimentalism,' as if it was scandalous and called into questions of the Englishman's character. Valencia Decarli was unbothered "Correct, Mister Pryce. There is a precise purpose for each of you being here. In the interest of your privacies, my father does not wish to address any issue with anyone apart from the man the issue is concerned with."

Cesar thought of the incident with Antonin Rocca and the Unione Corse two years ago and deliberated on what other 'issue of importance' there could be between him and Alexander Decarli. He cleared his throat and gestured to attract Valencia Decarli's attention "Respectfully, I am not aware of this 'issue of importance' that your father would like to speak to me about."

"Neither am I," Pietro Biassiano said loudly.

Valencia was undaunted. "Your concerns are understood and appreciated. Please bear in mind though, my father is a private and busy man. The eight of you are also busy men, but not nearly so private as he is. Therefore, for those of you unaware of any issue of importance. I suppose that it is an issue that you and father are both involved in, but his involvement is not known to you."

There was an ominous silence.

"I implore you not to judge him for such secrecy. He is simply accustomed to a way of doing things. I need not ask that you can all respect that."

Von Strichtenheimer had something to say, "Please forgive any rudeness that may be interpreted from my asking…But why is he not here instead of you?"

"Yes, I think we would all like to meet Alexander as soon as possible," Galopin said.

"I have the privilege of serving as a hostess for this event and addressing you honorable gentlemen on my father's behalf. Rest assured though, it is only so that I may make the introduction for the night. He is present at the hotel tonight, and he will be meeting us at what he believes to be the proper time."

"I would hope that all of us here understand as much,"

Rombauer said. "But we would like to know why your father did not consider now to be the proper time. Or why he would not simply meet us in the lobby as you had done?"

"I concur with Mister Rombauer" Dickerson said. "There must be some reasoning behind your father's actions for choosing to not meet us until a specified point?"

"I can promise you, knowing my father as I do, that his decision on when and where to join the party was not done for a reason that was frivolous or for the intention of insulting any man here. Once he reveals himself, I expect him to candidly explain himself."

Valencia allowed herself an amused chuckle. "Although I would not except an apology from him, he will explain the reasoning for what he does in the kindest possible manner, but I'm afraid he considers apologies to have no serious value."

The eight guests exchanged glances among each other.

"If you gentlemen are done with your drinks, then shall I request that you follow me to the Hotel's main dining room? My father will be waiting there for us. He, like the rest of you, is eager to proceed with what he has planned for tonight."

Chapter 3
Alexander the Great

The dining room that Valencia Decarli ushered Cesar and the other guests into was a beautiful old room that had escaped the renovation of the rest of the hotel. There was no ornate furnishing or decor. Instead, there were wooden floors, faded walls, and a great table that had seen many dinners. But it was not the room's appearance that attracted the attention of everyone present, it was the man who was standing in the room.

A dark-haired man wearing a dinner suit stood at one of the dining room windows and stared out at the Oesling countryside as daylight diminished and the dark dominion of the night approached. If he heard his daughter and guests enter the room, then he did not seem to think it was necessary that he direct his attention to them and instead continued to look out the window.

"Father" Valencia eventually said.

Alexander Decarli sighed audibly and tore himself away from the outside world to address his guests. He greeted them with a grin and then spoke "Ah-hah! Gentlemen, I had been wondering when my daughter would tire of charming you with her presence."

No one said anything. The eight men who had been summoned to the Hotel Geraldine by this enigmatic man could only regard him with bewilderment and curiosity now that they were finally confronted with him.

"Alexander Decarli" said a hard voice. It took Cesar a few

seconds to realize who had spoken, Sergei Melikov had been quiet until that point.

Decarli perked up at the sound of his own name "Sergei Simeonovich, it is plain to see that Copenhagen has been generous to you. You appear far younger than I expected you to."

Melikov did not welcome or reject this compliment and remained passively stoic.

The next person Decarli had eyes for was Felix von Strichtenheimer. "Mister Von Strichtenheimer. I look at you and I am reminded of a finer age. Not enough in our world have much remaining respect for lineage and the stories of great families."

Von Strichtenheimer nodded respectfully at him, but otherwise remained as stoic as Melikov. Decarli looked towards Galopin and moved towards him to shake his hand.

"Major Galopin, or Commandant as I believe it's called in your army. That is still your rank, yes?"

"To my current knowledge, I must make sure I still am one when I return to my post."

Decarli shook Pryce's hand. "Kenneth Pryce. I must compliment you on your photography and you're writing. Your recent article on the Paris Commune proved amusing to myself."

Pryce clearly wanted to retort but thought better of it "I… Thank you."

Decarli walked from Kenneth Pryce to Pietro Biassiano, as the two men were far away from each other.

"Pietro Biassiano" Decarli said while shaking his hand. "Ever a pleasure to have an Italian in my company. I fell in love with your peninsula during my earlier years, and I regret to admit I have not been back in some time."

"When you return you will find a transformed nation unfettered by the hindrances of western plutocracy and classist factionalism" Biassiano said pridefully.

Galopin glanced over at Biassiano severely. Pryce stared at the man as if he would've liked to physically hurt him. Dickerson exchanged an amused look with Cesar, as if Biassiano was not to be taken seriously. Cesar did not return the amusement.

Decarli gave Biassiano a patronizing smile and moved to shake Rombauer's hand.

"Ah, Doctor Rombauer. How are your colleagues in Gothenberg?"

"They are competent and predictable" Roherbach said in a self-satisfied tone.

"Ah, but is it not beneficial to be affiliated with those whose actions you are able to predict? I would imagine it to be even more the case when they're competent."

Rombauer gestured towards Decarli in acknowledgment that it was a sound point.

The last two men to receive Decarli's attention were Cesar and Dickerson, who both stood near each other "And at last, we have two sons of the Americas. Francis Edmund Dickerson and Cesar Mondragon."

Decarli shook Dickerson's hand "How is your Mister Roosevelt?"

"Dreadfully busy these days I'm afraid. He has plans for a third term, which if he is successful, will make him the first President to get one. I think Vice President Garner and James Farley at the DNC have other plans though."

"May fortune favor him."

Without moving away from Dickerson, Decarli looked over at Cesar "And you must be Cesar Mondragon" he said with a tone of simple finality.

"I am."

"Excellent, excellent" Decarli said quickly as he turned away from Cesar and addressed the assembled guests.

"Please gentlemen, sit. You are all uncertain of me, and as you should be, I might add. Though I see no reason why we cannot have dinner while you are uncertain. We've taken the liberty of assigning you seats, which I hope is only a small bother to you."

On the side of the table near the windows, Biassiano, Dickerson, Galopin, and Melikov sat down at the seats where their surnames were written down. Cesar found his own name of "Mondragon" on the side of the table away from the windows, and sat down next to Pryce, Rombauer, von Strichtenheimer.

Alexander and his daughter each sat on opposite ends of the table. Him between Biassiano and Cesar, her between Melikov and Von Strichtenheimer.

Once all ten of them were seated, Alexander grabbed a small bell that sat on the table and rang it gently. A few moments passed before a man in a butler's uniform emerged from the dining room's service door.

"Christoph" Decarli said cordially, as if the butler was his good friend. "We are a ready for our dinner service."

"Very good."

Christoph went back through the service door. Not a minute had passed when a line of servers came out with their food. The main dish was an Oesling ham served with potatoes and salad. Placed on one side of the ham was a platter of French breads and cheeses. On the other side of the ham was a bowl of assorted fruits. Finally, pitchers of wine, milk, and water were brought out last for refreshments.

The meal was eaten quietly. None of the dinner guests were evidently aware of their business here, and they were all suspicious of Decarli. It was not surprising then that they had little desire to speak to each other. Valencia, however, was still determined to play the hostess.

"Mister Pryce, is it true you are from Gloucestershire?"

Kenneth Pryce finished chewing his food before answering "I am yes, thank you for asking."

"Is that near Wiltshire?"

"Wiltshire is south of Gloucestershire."

"Father and I once knew a man from Wiltshire. His name was Cleverly if I recall. Do you know who I'm talking about father?"

"Vaguely," Alexander responded.

Pryce cleared his throat "Sadly, I haven't been back to Gloucestershire at any recent date."

"Where do you live presently?" Valencia asked.

"I have a flat in Paris that I haven't been to in months. My last residence was a rented room in Bastogne. My work affords me a vagabond lifestyle."

"Oh I see, rather like Mister Mondragon."

Cesar looked up, startled to hear his name.

Valencia saw that Cesar was startled and appeared to think it was something she said. "I forgot to ask, do you prefer Mister Mondragon or Senor Mondragon? Or would you prefer Cesar?"

"I don't have a preference" Cesar said uncertainly.

"I shall you call Cesar."

"You were saying something about me and Cesar?" Pryce said to Valencia.

"Yes of course!" She looked back to Cesar. "You and Mister Pryce are both well-traveled men and have seen much of Europe. Or am I mistaken?"

Cesar felt more than a few pairs of eyes on him "I live in England where Mister Pryce is from, but yes I do travel."

"And you originally came from Mexico."

He stared at Valencia, who simply sat and looked at him serenely as she waited for an answer.

"I was born there if that's what you're asking."

"Is it true you fought in the Mexican Revolution?"

He almost choked on the water he was drinking. Remaining calm, he placed his glass down and hastily assessed his options. He couldn't refuse to respond, and it was clear that Alexander and Valencia already knew who he was, so he just told the truth. "I joined the Constitutional Army when I was a young man."

Valencia acted interested, but how genuine her interest was suspect. "Fascinating, tell me more about this Constitutional Army."

"You want me to tell you about the Constitutional Army?" Cesar asked, blinking in puzzlement.

"Mm-hmm."

Cesar paused as he thought of what to say. "The Constitutional Army was formed after the overthrow and murder of President Francisco Madero, and its purpose was to preserve the revolution by fighting the dictatorship of Victoriano Huerta."

He thought he sounded like a historian as opposed to someone that had been there, but he had little proficiency for pleasant conversation, even less so when the topic of conversation was something so personal to him.

"One of Carranza's boys, eh?" Dickerson said, enthusiastically joining the conversation. "You fought that scoundrel Huerta and his people, did you?"

"Initially yes, but after Huerta's people, it was Pancho Villa and Zapata's people that we fought."

"Didn't the late German Empire supply weapons to Huerta's forces?"

Everyone looked in Decarli's direction, his unexpected entry into the conversation capturing their attention instantly.

Cesar saw that Decarli was looking at him, and assumed he was the one the question was directed towards "I don't...Are you asking me, or..."

"I do believe they did," Decarli asserted. "Doctor Rombauer..."

Rombauer's head rose, giving him the appearance of an alert, elderly dog.

"Your work in armaments research and engineering for the *Kaiserreich* predates Huerta. Perhaps weapons whose development you contributed to were used to kill Mister Mondragon's colleagues?

Rombauer was silently dumbstruck. He didn't seem upset, but he was clearly not expecting the conversation to take this turn and was at a loss for how to conduct himself.

Decarli drank some wine as he received many strange looks,

Cesar himself wasn't looking at Decarli, but rather at his plate as he tangled with his assorted thoughts. He was astute enough to realize that Decarli was trying to provoke him, to extract some reaction from him. What surprised him was the blatantness with which it was done, the flippancy that Decarli displayed when referencing the most formative event of Cesar's youth and the needless death it caused.

And what for? To test him? To disrespect him? Perhaps to mock him for so willingly coming to Luxembourg to eat dinner with people he didn't know?

"Mexico…" Cesar eventually started to say, still avoiding eye contact with anyone.

"Yes, Mexico what, Mister Mondragon?" Decarli asked, having the tone of a bored professor leading a class.

Cesar looked at Decarli and found the words he needed.

"Mexico's Revolution was fought with guns from all manner of nations. Many of which changed hands several times. I can't claim to know how many of the guns that killed my fellow Constitutionalists were from Germany or otherwise."

He then looked at Rombauer as if to apologize on behalf of Decarli. "If Doctor Rombauer played some small indirect role in the suffering of my country than I know better than to blame him for it."

Cesar and Rombauer held each other's gaze for a moment, the clarity of what he said quite plain. They both directed their attention back to their host.

Decarli, who had cordially been listening to Cesar with his hands clasped together, smiled pleasantly. "I'll confess I know precious little about it," he gestured towards Cesar as if to acquiesce to him.

The room was once more silent, but it was a much louder silence than before. Decarli was looking out the window again, his expression melancholy.

"Erm…You were a revolutionary then?" Pryce said, hoping to move the conversation forward.

"That's a matter of perspective" Cesar said humbly "Villa and Zapata's men would've told you that they were the revolutionaries. Maybe Huerta's men thought the same."

"This war you fought in doesn't make any sense!" Biassiano said suddenly in a bombastic voice. Everyone at the table either glanced over at him with disdain or avoided looking at him.

"Wars seldom do" Cesar said simply.

"Nonsense, I fought in a war that made sense. My fellow Italians and I fought Germany and Austria-Hungary. We were united as a singular people and achieved a great victory. Land that was rightfully ours, but belonged to our enemies, was returned to us. And we would've received more if not for the interference of the other European powers."

Everyone in the room had stopped eating and was sitting frozen. It was not because of what Biassiano said though, it was because of von Strichtenheimer, who was sitting in his chair and staring at no one with a vacant expression. Cesar, who was sitting a few chairs away from the Austrian nobleman, could intuitively sense the anger and hatred emitting from him.

Alexander Decarli noticed this and broke into a trickster's grin. He had been testing the waters before with Cesar and Rombauer, but now he was ready "Mister von Strichtenheimer, as an Austrian, you must have some opinion on the subject?"

The room became incredibly tense. Biassiano wore a surprised expression, as if he only just remembered he was sharing the dinner table with Austrian nobility. His surprise was soon replaced by callousness as he leered over at von Strichtenheimer "I too, would like to hear von Strichtenheimer's opinion."

Von Strichtenheimer looked at Decarli and spoke in a voice that was frighteningly cold. "The Italians have never had the pleasure of fighting the Austrian Nation at its full strength. When they fought my people, they not only did so with the patronage of those European powers that Mister Biassiano seems to resent, but with the Balkan region causing no end of trouble to the empire. A fair fight between Austria and Italy would've resulted in the latter's destruction."

"That is a theory I pray will one day be tested" Biassiano said smugly as he examined the bottom of his empty glass, as if to imply it was of greater interest than anyone who was speaking to him.

Alexander, clearly enjoying himself, decided to make another remark "Mister Biassiano, were you aware that two of Mister von Strichtenheimer's brothers were killed —"

"Father!" Valencia interjected, but Alexander didn't stop.

" — fighting in Italy during the same theatre you fought in?"

Biassiano laughed sadistically "If they were, then I can only hope that it was Italian guns that killed them."

Von Strichtenheimer stood up from his chair, Rombauer made an effort to grab his arm, but he was thrown off by him. He moved around the end of the table.

"Mister von Stricht-" Valencia tried to say to von Strichtenheimer as he passed her, but it was in vain.

Von Strichtenheimer was intercepted by Melikov who had stood up to grab him and was now holding him against the wall "Let me go!"

Biassiano had also stood up from his chair and was being restrained by Galopin.

"Out of my way you fool!" Biassiano barked.

"Shall I make a cretin out of you for nothing?" Galopin said slickly.

Pryce ran to the other side of the table to aid Galopin in holding back Biassiano.

"Sit down" Galopin growled to Biassiano.

"Did you just give me an order *Franchese?*"

"Yes, I have!" Galopin said fiercely.

"Do as he tells you" Pryce snapped "If anyone will cave in your fascist skull it will be myself."

Biassiano relented and sat down in his chair, but not before speaking Italian to Pryce "*Non puoi fermare il nuovo ordine, socialista.*"

Pryce surprised Biassiano by responding in the same language "*Non vedo l'ora di provare.*"

Biassiano dismissed Pryce with disdainful snicker and proceeded to gaze around the room imperiously. Von Strichtenheimer finally managed to overpower Melikov, but he was stopped by Galopin who held out one strong arm in front of him.

"Return to your seat" Galopin said with deadly seriousness.

"My family has been insulted."

Cesar could tell that rage was building beneath Galopin's cold exterior "I told you to return to your seat."

Von Strichtenheimer seethed "You will not-"

Galopin silenced him with a severe look. Von Strichtenheimer did not appear to be afraid, but he was at a loss for words.

"Do you think you're the only one?" Galopin eventually asked, his tone grave.

Galopin and Von Strichtenheimer stared each other down, determining each other through their eyes. All present in the room watched them with rapt attention. Eventually Von Strichtenheimer woodenly turned away, retraced his path around the table, and then gently took his seat. Pryce and Melikov also took their seats once they were certain Biassiano and von Strichtenheimer would not be standing up again.

Galopin remained standing as if expecting to subdue any other person who dared make another attempt of disrupting the dinner. After a few moments, the service door opened, and Christoph peaked into the room, a look of concern on his face.

Decarli noticed him and gave him a reassuring smile.

"Everything is quite alright Christoph. A disagreement, men of pride and a fair amount of wine, that sort of thing."

Christoph remained in place for a few moments before disappearing from sight.

Galopin had begun to stare at Decarli with a look of great incredulity and contempt.

"Decarli!"

"Hmm?"

"Is this a spectacle to you?"

Decarli feigned confusion, it was a convincing display of confusion, but Cesar's estimation of this man was that he was far smarter than he led others to believe, and that confusion did not come naturally to him "I'm afraid I do not know what you mean."

"What are we doing here?"

"As Valencia and I have both explained-"

"I am not interested in your pleasantries! I am interested in what you intend by this tactic."

"And what tactic is that?"

"I am not an unintelligent man. This is a masquerade, but the only one wearing a mask is you."

"Major Galopin-"

"Do not speak!" Galopin thundered. "Unless you wish to tell me what you will have with us, then I am no longer interested in your words."

Decarli rested his head against the back of his chair and closed his eyes for several long moments. When he opened them again, he looked towards Galopin with as much respect as he could muster "I have decided to respect your wishes, Galopin. If you will kindly be seated, I shall forgo all formal obligations in the interest of expediency and divulge information that I trust will make sense of this event."

Galopin hesitated, as if he wanted to keep arguing, but then he went back to his chair and sat down heavily.

With all seated, Decarli sat up in his chair so that all at the table could see and hear him "Gentlemen, I have not long for this world."

The eight guests were not as surprised by this news as they were confused and indifferent. Valencia had her hands folded in front of her and was gazing downward solemnly. Alexander continued.

"I will not go into unnecessary details, but I suspect that by the end of the next summer, I will be dead. When I told you that there was matter I had to discuss with each of you, I was telling the truth. As my remaining time is limited and therefore must be rationed, I thought it necessary to bring you all to one place so that things may be settled quickly and efficiently. The secrecy was out of respect for you, I did not want any man to be aware of another man's personal business.

"Misters von Strichtenheimer and Biassiano, I apologize for provoking your patriotic sensibilities. I'm afraid such petty games are a source of levity to myself now that I am at the end of my life. I would not presume to ask for your forgiveness though. By all means take issue with me, but do not dwell on it."

Decarli sighed as he stopped speaking. The room was quiet for a few moments.

"We continue to hear about you having to discuss a personal matter with us" Melikov said. "I think we would all like to know what these matters are."

Melikov received strange looks. This was only the second time he had spoken, and it was still jarring to hear him speak.

Decarli purposefully stood up from his chair. "Yes, thank you Mister Melikov, you are absolutely right. Clearly our appetites our modest tonight, therefore I think our dinner service is concluded. Please follow me and Valencia. We are to return the hotel's drawing room. All is to be explained upon our arrival."

Chapter 4
An Unexpected Development

The same drawing room they had originally gathered in was where they returned after dinner. Alexander Decarli and his daughter entered first, with Cesar and the other guests following behind then. Alexander waited until everyone had entered before speaking.

"Gentlemen, if you would look to my right, you will notice a door at the end of the room. This leads to another room where I will be meeting with each of you one by one, and during which I will discuss the reasons for having brought you here. I will be meeting with Doctor Rombauer first, Major Galopin second, Mister Pryce third, Mister Von Strichtenheimer fourth, Mister Melikov fifth, Mister Dickerson sixth, Mister Biassiano seventh, and Mister Mondragon eighth."

"Is there a reason for this particular order?" Galopin asked.

"It is simply the order I've decided on..." Alexander said curtly, "and I'm unwilling to divert from it, I take my decisions quite seriously."

He looked around as if daring anyone to challenge this, no one did.

"Beloved Valencia?"

"Yes, father?"

"Remain here with them, won't you my darling?"

"I shall, father. Thank you."

The father and daughter stared at each other for a few strange moments, but then Alexander looked away from her "Doctor Rombauer, if you will walk with me."

Decarli and Rombauer went to the side room for their meeting. Cesar noticed a peculiar expression on Valencia's face as her father walked away from her, it was difficult to comprehend and vanished far quicker than it had appeared.

With his meeting with Decarli scheduled last, Cesar found a chair to sit in. He pulled his journal and a pencil from his coat and began to write down the names of every individual who was present tonight, along with his own thoughts on them.

> *Alexander Decarli. The one who brought us here. Wealthy and secretive. Fond of demonstrating aristocratic eloquence and poise, but it is almost certainly an affectation. Mischievous at the best, malevolent at the worst.*
>
> *Valencia Decarli. Outgoing, confident, shares her father's eloquence. Uncertain if she's of an equivalent standard to her father, or if she is his unwitting asset.*
>
> *Francis Dickerson. Affable, the only one who enjoys being here. He either has no secrets or is adept at concealing them.*
>
> *Kenneth Pryce. Disheveled, looks out of place. He has the eyes of someone who's seen terrible things.*
>
> *Dieudonne Galopin. A hardened man, weary but domineering. He will take command of a situation if he is compelled to.*
>
> *Ludwig Rombauer. Oblivious, cumbersome conversationalist. He has the appearance and demeanor of one who enjoys a hermitic existence. Probably harmless.*
>
> *Felix von Strichtenheimer. Young and hotheaded. Imbued with a nobleman's pride and lack of restraint, possibly unpredictable.*
>
> *Sergei Melikov. Quiet, avoids eye contact, hard to analyze.*
>
> *Pietro Biassiano. Enthusiastic fascist, bellicose, prideful, unconcerned with what others think or if he upsets them.*

As the meetings continued, Cesar observed that they each lasted for an approximate duration of ten minutes. Eight ten-minute meetings meant that the entire ordeal would take eighty minutes to complete. This was confirmed when Dickerson finished his meeting with Decarli at the sixty-minute marker. Biassiano was next, which meant that in ten minutes Cesar would have his meeting and would finally be able to ascertain answers from Decarli. He expected the man to be resistant and to use his powers of personality and rhetoric as a defense mechanism.

It wasn't going to work, Cesar would get what he was looking for.

As Biassiano ventured through the door to the side room where Decarli was, Cesar took the time to survey the other guests around him. Rombauer and Von Strichtenheimer were quietly conversing with each other in German, but were soon interrupted by Dickerson, who had felt the need to insert himself into their conversation and began speaking English. Melikov sat by himself and had the look of being deep in thought. Pryce sat on a sofa and was reading from a book that had been sitting on a table. Near Pryce was Galopin, who paced about with his hands folded behind his back.

Valencia Decarli was still eager to play the hostess and effortlessly navigated the room, striking up conversations with the various guests and then departing once the conversations were exhausted. Cesar was the only one she hadn't spoken to at least once, he was rather surprised by this and expected that she would soon be speaking to him. In a few minutes, his expectation was met.

"I beg your pardon Cesar…Would it be rude if I were to ask what you're writing?"

"My thoughts."

"Ah excellent, would your thoughts be disturbed if I were to sit with you?"

"Not at all."

She took the seat opposite him.

"I apologize that my father deigned to meet with you last. I promise it was not his wish to be disrespectful, or to suggest that your business with him is less important when compared to the others here."

Cesar did not look up from his journal "What was your father's reason for meeting with his guests in a such a specific fashion?"

"He did not think to tell me, and it was not my desire to ask him. He habitually relies on intuition and whims, vexatious of him really, but nothing quite so pernicious has come of it, therefore it is tolerable."

"Do you know anything of the matter your father wants to speak to me about?"

"Are you inquiring as to whether I know? Or are you requesting that I tell you what I certainly do know?"

Cesar looked up from his journal at her, taken aback by this response. Valencia calmly stared at him.

"I…I am asking you whether or not you know."

"I'm afraid that I do not and wish that I did, as I would gladly share the information with you now that you're meeting with him is in a few minutes."

She frowned suddenly "Oh, please forgive me."

"Forgive you for what?"

"I have played the dominant role in this conversation, even though this was not my intention. My intention was for you to speak more, so that I may gain insight into your thought process."

He looked at her "And why would you gain insight into thought process?"

She smiled and shrugged "I suppose it's because of my fondness for people and their intricacies. The way someone thinks is quite fascinating to me."

"I'd rather guard against any insight you might gain into my thought process."

She did not seem offended, and instead raised one of her eyebrows at him "You assume that I'm untrustworthy? That it would be against your own interest and wellbeing to open yourself up to me?"

"To be honest Miss Decarli, I have no idea what to assume. I've come a long way to attend this function, and even though I've been here for some length of time, I still don't know the reason for it other than this nebulous business your father has with me."

"I understand your position, and I hope you don't find that I'm unsympathetic. Though I must ask if it's fair that you assume the worst of my father and I? Have we not been courteous to you? You are a guest of this hotel, and you were provided with dinner, and at no expense to yourself. Surely you wouldn't deem this kindness to be irrelevant?"

Cesar closed his journal and concealed it within his coat, he gave her his full attention. "What would 'assuming the worst' be?"

"I beg your pardon?"

"You asked if it's fair for me to assume the worst of you and your father? What would 'assuming the worst' be?"

For the first time that night, Valencia Decarli was at a loss for a line. She blinked a few times as she thought of a response – and then the door to the side room opened.

Biassiano emerged from the side room with a dour look on his face, all looked towards him with surprise as ten minutes had not passed. "There is something wrong with Decarli" he announced indelicately.

"What are you talking about?" Galopin asked loudly.

"He's on the ground and he is not moving."

No sooner than Biassiano had finished speaking was Valencia on her feet and running towards the room her father was in. Cesar hesitated for a moment, before jumping out of his chair and following her. Biassiano silently moved out of the way of Valencia and Cesar as they went through the door he had come out of.

The side room was much smaller than the drawing room. The walls and floors were both made of stone and there was a table and chairs illuminated by a single hanging lamp. Lying on the floor next to the table was the convulsing and choking form of Alexander Decarli.

"Father!" Valencia cried out, immediately at his side.

"Valencia" he struggled to say through the bile he was choking on.

"Father…" she said breathlessly while fighting back tears. "I… I…"

Alexander put his hand on her face, and she fell silent immediately. His choking grew worse, he made a sound that Cesar recognized as a death rattle, and then his hand fell from his daughter's face. He didn't move or make any sound after that. Valencia sobbed softly over her father's body.

As Cesar began to fully grasp what he had just witnessed, he was struck by Valencia's grief and how quickly it came. Cesar had seen enough death to know how people reacted to it: There was shock, denial, hysteria, but there was none of that with Valencia. She immediately understood the situation and had accepted it.

Cesar believed it resembled the behavior of someone sitting next to a loved one on a sick bed, not someone who in less than a minute had both discovered their father was dying and watched him die. He was unsure, but one conclusion came to him, and his first instinct was to test it.

"You knew this was going to happen," Cesar said coolly to her.

She turned her head halfway in his direction but did not look at him, this only confirmed Cesar's suspicion.

Before Cesar could say anything else, Galopin entered the room.

"What has happened?" he asked, looking at Valencia and her father's body on the floor.

"Mister Decarli has died" Cesar explained.

"What did you say?" Galopin gaped at him, his hard-blue eyes wide. He looked at Decarli's recently deceased person and realized it was true. "How is this possible? Died of what?"

"I don't know" Cesar answered.

Francis Edmund Dickerson entered next, followed by Kenneth Pryce. Galopin quickly addressed them. "Pryce, Dickerson, a terrible thing has happened. Decarli is dead."

"Good God" Dickerson said with quiet horror. Pryce had an uneasy expression.

Galopin took charge "Pryce, inform the other four that Decarli is dead."

Pryce briefly looked at Decarli's body before leaving to carry out Galopin's instructions.

"Dickerson, if you would, please remove Miss Decarli from this room."

"Remove her? ... Yes of course."

Dickerson helped Valencia off the floor. "Come along dear" he said gently "Your father's better off now."

Galopin waited till Dickerson and Valencia were gone before speaking to Cesar "What happened to Alexander Decarli?"

"I've already said that I don't know."

"You will not lie to me" Galopin said, more forcefully than before.

Cesar glared at Galopin irately "Do you mean to accuse me of something?"

"Why do you have a revolver in your coat?" He grinned as Cesar's surprise "Yes, I noticed it. I know who you are *mon ami.* Your reputation in France is greater than you assume it to be."

Cesar remained quiet.

"You are skeptical? Then allow me to name affairs you were involved in. That killer that lured his victims into the catacombs in Paris? That widow in Calais with the missing son? And what of the spring of last year when you were in Romania? I only know what I heard and what I heard was most strange."

"But of course, I should hope not to forget about that business with a fugitive two years ago, business which was connected to the Corsican syndicates as well as the man who now lies dead before us.

"I see from your expression that I have perplexed you. I shall ask a question that will hopefully be less perplexing. If your reputation is to be taken seriously, then I expect you to have a semblance of an idea of how this man died. Now I will ask only once more: What happened to Decarli?"

Cesar stared at Galopin, but the man showed no signs of relenting. Not knowing what else to do, he looked around the room. There wasn't much to see, but one of the first things that caught Cesar's eye was a pitcher of water and an empty glass on the table. He looked at Decarli's body and noticed broken glass not far from where he lay. It dawned on Cesar that Decarli had fallen to the ground while holding the second glass, and it shattered upon impact with the stone floor. This information, along with the coughing and convulsion exhibited by Decarli, led Cesar to a simple conclusion.

"Perhaps he was poisoned."

Galopin looked at Decarli's body, then at the pitcher of water on the table, and then back at Cesar. If he thought the answer was plausible, then he did not make it known through his facial expression.

"Hand me your revolver" he ordered.

Cesar saw no way out of it and calming surrendered his LeMat revolver to Galopin

"Mister Mondragon, will you please walk with me back to the main room?" he requested formally.

The two of them walked back into the drawing room. The guests were all standing and in animated conversation with each other. Valencia sat by herself, a pensive expression on her face as her tears dried.

"It couldn't have been his disease" Pryce said.

"Why not?" Von Strichtenheimer asked.

"He told us at dinner he suspected that he'd be dead within a year, not dead within the night," Pryce explained.

"Perhaps he lied" Rombauer suggested.

"For what reason?" Dickerson said bewildered "What could possibly be the point of lying about how long he had to live and then dying this very night? Because he thought it would be funny?"

"Quiet!" Galopin shouted. "A man has died here. Until we understand why he died, nobody is leaving this room."

While Galopin spoke, Cesar carefully positioned himself behind him. Convinced that the French Major was unaware of his being behind him, Cesar grabbed an antique chair with both hands and swung it into the man's back. The chair broke apart and Galopin fell to the ground heavily.

The guests all erupted in exclamations of shock and confusion at Cesar's sudden act of violence.

"What the *hell* are you doing?" Pryce exploded as he rounded on Cesar.

He quickly retrieved his LeMat revolver from Galopin's hand and pointed it at the approaching Englishman. Pryce stopped dead in his tracks as he saw that Cesar was armed and raised his hands defensively.

"Will the one responsible for the murder of Alexander Decarli please reveal themselves?" Cesar said casually.

The response to this was shocked silence. Galopin slowly stood up from the ground, Cesar pointed the gun towards him to keep him at bay. Galopin stood tall and looked at Cesar with an expression of tranquil power "What is it you believe you are doing?" he asked in a dangerously low voice.

"I am determining who killed Decarli" Cesar said firmly.

"By asking the guilty party to reveal themselves?" Galopin snapped.

"I had hoped that the killer would expose themselves through their reaction."

"And did they?"

"No," Cesar said with a sigh.

"What leads you to believe that he was murdered?" Dickerson asked.

"The way in which he died, the broken glass, and the pitcher of water; all of it points to him being poisoned. As he met with the seven of you before dying, I infer that one of you poisoned him."

"Why would we want to poison him?" Biassiano asked.

"That's what I aspire to find out" Cesar said.

"The Italian was the last one to meet with him!" Von Strichtenheimer said, pointing at Biassiano. "He must've poisoned him!"

"Slander," Biassiano barked.

"It would've not been the first time you murdered defenseless people Pietro," Pryce said with a great deal of contempt.

"Enough of this" Galopin said calmly "This gets us nowhere. Mister Mondragon said he wishes to determine who killed Decarli. He and I share the same objective."

"Mister Mondragon attacked you with a chair" Dickerson pointed out plainly.

Galopin made a dismissive gesture "Has my ego been wounded? *Naturellement,* but my reason remains intact. My estimation of Mister Mondragon is that he is are not a man of vulgarity or bravado, it would contradict his character for him to strike me with that chair unless he believed that I was able to withstand such a thing" He brushed a splinter from the chair off himself. "He was correct by the way."

Galopin turned his attention to Cesar. He stood up straight and spoke in a formative voice "If conflict between you and I is inevitable, then I call on God as the only force which can stop this. Regardless, no action will be taken unless inevitability is a certainty. Until then, we will conduct our inquires separately."

Cesar nodded "Understood." He then spoke loudly enough for all to hear him "I believe it best, if all who met with Decarli revealed the details of the purported business he had with them."

There were few objections, and it was agreed upon. The seven who had their meetings with Decarli before his death all made known what his business was with them.

Rombauer, as the first to meet with Decarli, was the first to talk. He spoke nervously, still very startled by all that had happened. "The Swiss government would like for myself to relocate to their country. With another war in Europe possible, they have been accelerating military development in the pursuit of a policy of armed neutrality. They believe my past in military engineering would prove useful and Decarli served as their representative in this matter. I was promised terms more favorable than the ones I currently have in Gothenberg. However now that Decarli has died, I am uncertain what becomes of the offer."

Galopin crossed his arms and spoke with his usual forthcoming bluntness "Decarli had a list of officers in the French military who I have quarreled with before, and he had evidence of scandalous behavior involving them, the type of behavior that could uproot one's career. He thought I could make use of it. Few things would've pleased me as much as to be rid of these imbeciles who call themselves my fellow officers, but as Doctor Rombauer has said, Decarli's death puts the prospect in question."

Pryce was oddly calm as he spoke "He had sensitive photographs and documents that were entrusted to him years ago by a man who was a Bolshevik. The photos and documents revealed various wrongdoings and injustices perpetrated by the late Tsar's government and the White Army during the Russian Civil War. As it happens, this old revolutionary was arrested last year by Stalin's internal security forces and isn't expected to be heard from again, so Decarli needed someone to entrust the items to. Given that many in the west despise the Soviet government, he thought they were best entrusted to a left-wing journalist. I was the one he chose."

Von Strichtenheimer avoided looking at anybody and instead stared at his hands as if he just realized he had them, he spoke in a smooth and glossy voice and was as calm as Pryce. "As you are aware, Germany annexed my home country of Austria last year. Many Austrians, either currently living in Austria or residing in foreign lands were and remain opposed to it, but they were in no position to challenge the will of Hitler's government in Berlin. Decarli agreed with this opposition and sought to actively undermine the incorporation of Austria into Germany. He wondered if I might make introductions to other Austrians who would be useful in achieving this aim. However, I informed him that I was neutral towards the annexation, having not lived in Austria for quite some time."

Melikov's mannerisms were as stoic as they had been all night. "For reasons that he did not wish to make known to me, Mister Decarli wanted to open lines of communication with extended family members of Maria Feodorovna, the late Empress of Russia and Danish princess. I do not know any of these family members, but I am affiliated with people who do know them. And that it is why I was invited here."

Dickerson cleared his throat and did his best to speak in a plain, conversational tone, but he shared some of Rombauer's nervousness. "Yes, well…Even though he was first and foremost a European businessman, Decarli had business interests in America, but he did not trust his European associates to look after them once he died. He claimed to be conscious of the differences between Americans and Europeans, and therefore felt an American entrepreneur was better suited to oversee his affairs on the other side of the Atlantic. He would've sold whatever he owned in America to myself, and then I would've been free to sell to other

Americans or keep what I thought was worth keeping."

Biassiano stuck his chin out and spoke with officious bombast, as if he was delivering a proclamation "During the Great War, Switzerland was a destination for deserters from the Royal Italian Army. Many of these deserters were also thieves, they brought with them to Switzerland artifacts they had stolen from museums and private collections. Artifacts of value to the dignity and cultural heritage of the Italian people, but the only value these deserters found in them was the price they fetched on the black market" He spit on the ground to register his disgust. "Decarli was noble enough to devote time to gathering these items with the intent of returning them to *Italia*. I was to inform Rome of his intentions, but before he could say more or tell me what artifacts he had, he fell on the floor and began to die." Biassiano smiled, greatly pleased with his abrupt and tactless ending.

As each man spoke, Cesar sat at a table and wrote the relevant parts in his journal. Once done, he closed his journal and stood up to address the room. "Let me make this plain: I have not the ability nor the desire to hold anyone here against their will. All who wish to leave the hotel are free to do so, I will not impede them. My intention from this point is to accumulate information. I seek to know who killed Decarli, and what his reason was for bringing us here."

"He already told each of us why he wanted us here," Rombauer said. "With the exception of you Mister Mondragon."

Cesar had a question prepared "How many of you believe, that the reason he gave you, is the real reason you're here?"

They exchanged a few looks with one another, but nobody said anything. Evidently, none of them was convinced of Decarli's explanation for what their purpose was at the Hotel Geraldine.

"I'm pleased to see it wasn't just me then..." Cesar said.

"I shall be retiring to my room" Biassiano said, standing up and exiting the drawing room without another glance at anyone.

"As shall I" Melikov said, following suit.

The rest of them were content to stay grouped together in the drawing room.

"Anyone else have something to say?" Cesar asked.

"What should be done with Decarli's body?" Pryce wondered.

"Please, leave him" Valencia said, speaking for the first time since she had watched her father die. "I will have someone come for him."

"Mister Pryce" Galopin said suddenly. "I would like to speak with you in private."

"Concerning what?" questioned Pryce.

"It must be in private."

Pryce appeared concerned, but not terribly troubled, and went out into the hallway with Galopin.

The only ones left in the room were Cesar, Dickerson, Rombauer, Von Strichtenheimer, and of course Valencia Decarli. Dickerson and Rombauer found two chairs to sit in and began to quietly speak to each other. Von Strichtenheimer closed the door to the room that Decarli's body was in and stood still for a few seconds, his head facing the door. Cesar observed him.

Without saying a word or looking at anyone, Von Strichtenheimer walked casually over to the drawing room's spiral staircase and went up it to the second floor.

"Cesar."

He turned to see Valencia Decarli standing next to him.

"I would like to be of assistance to you."

"Assistance?"

"Yes, you said that you wanted to know who killed my father, I too want to know this."

Cesar frowned at her "What makes you think that you could be of assistance to me?"

She raised her hands to gesture towards her surroundings "I've been coming to the Geraldine all my life. I know the location of every room and corridor. And despite its vast size, my father only made use of a small selection of its faculties. I imagine you will want to see those faculties."

Cesar was wary of Decarli's daughter, and he strongly doubted she was just as clueless about her father's death as he was, but he was also in no position to turn down such a valuable source of useful information "You are welcome to assist me, but I must warn you, if I find out that you are in anyway hampering my efforts to gather information on what has taken place here tonight, then your 'assistance' will be at an end."

"You don't trust me?" she said as if she was offended.

"Should I?"

She did not answer. "Please follow me" she said to Cesar as she walked towards the drawing room's main door.

"Where are we going?" he asked.

"A number of locations" she said vaguely.

"Such as?" he asked incredulously, but she had already left the room. He walked after her but was distracted by the sound of his own name.

"Mister Mondragon?"

Cesar looked to see Dickerson walking towards him.

"So sorry sir. I wonder if I might have a word?"

"Concerning?"

Dickerson briefly scanned around the room. The only person left in the room was Rombauer, who was sitting in an armchair away from any door and looking around as if he was scanning the room for an axe murderer.

Once the American was satisfied that no one was eavesdropping, he turned back to Cesar "It's about Biassiano. If you're going to be getting to the bottom of things around here, I'd be weary of him."

Cesar was intrigued and suspicious of this warning, His instinct was to keep Dickerson talking. "And why is that?"

Dickerson raised one of his eyebrows "You mean apart from him being a vulgar specimen?"

Cesar stared at him "Additional reasons would be helpful, yes."

"I did my research on my fellow guests before I came, I'm sure I wasn't the only one…"

Cesar had an urge to say, *"you weren't,"* but he wasn't going to confirm nor deny any of Dickerson's suspicions if he didn't have to.

"…And my research turned up disconcerting details on Biassiano."

"What details?"

"Details about activities that aren't part of his duties as a Prefect of Italy. This isn't the first time he's ventured outside his nation. He does it quite often, much too often for a man whose occupation with the Fascist government is strictly provincial…If you get my meaning."

Cesar did get his meaning. Italian prefects were supposed to represent the state and coordinate the police in their provinces. It was unnecessary and impractical for them to routinely travel elsewhere.

"Where does he go when he leaves Italy?" Cesar asked slowly and clearly, as if it were his only chance to ask the question.

Dickerson adjusted his glasses and cleared his throat "Well now…That would be getting to the point where I'd have to slander a man without hard evidence…I will say though, that he has some interesting friends, not just among his comrades in Rome…But in Rome's new ally to the north."

Cesar took a page from Dickerson's book and looked around to make sure nobody had entered the room before he asked his next question "Do you think he killed Decarli?"

"I don't know, and I can't say why he would either. I suppose it's possible the Fascists had a reason to want Decarli dead. But if that was so, it seems odd that Decarli would invite him here."

"This entire event is odd Mister Dickerson."

"Cesar, are you coming?"

He looked to where Valencia stood in the drawing room door "Just a moment."

He spoke quietly so only Dickerson could hear him. "What of his daughter? Should I be cautious of her?"

"She seems friendly enough, but I wouldn't trust anyone here sir, and that includes myself. I only wish to warn you about Biassiano."

"And now you've done so."

Dickerson saw that Cesar regarded their conversation as over and nodded solemnly to him. The American turned away from Cesar and walked across the room to where Rombauer sat.

"Ah! Mister Rombauer! Quite a bit of excitement, yes?"

Cesar left the drawing room to find Valencia waiting for him in the corridor.

"What did Mister Dickerson want?"

Cesar glanced at her unforthcomingly and thought of the best way to communicate his distrust to her. But she beat him to it. "Oh, I do beg your pardon. That was somewhat of an intrusive question, wasn't it?"

"Only somewhat," he quipped.

Valencia beamed at him. "Very well, I trust that if what you and he talked about was of any importance to me, I shall learn about it at that proper moment."

She spoke so pleasantly that one couldn't help but think it was inappropriate. Her father had died in her arms not more than thirty minutes ago and she was now carrying on merrily as if she was still hosting a party. Was this her way of grieving? Was she even grieving?

"Ah, but that's quite enough of my loquaciousness. Come Cesar, follow me."

With few other courses of action available, Cesar followed her.

An Event in Luxembourg

ACT

II

Chapter 5
A Theft of Keys

The Hotel Geraldine had a doctor on staff. The first location that Valencia led Cesar to had been the staff room, where she met with the doctor. She informed him of her father's death and requested that he examine the body. She also, on Cesar's advice, told the doctor to check the contents of the glass pitcher. While this meeting took place, Cesar waited in the corridor outside and eavesdropped at the door. He had no reason to believe that Valencia's conversation with the doctor would reveal any useful information, but it was a habit of Cesar to listen to private conversations.

When he heard someone approaching the door, he moved away and leaned inconspicuously against the adjacent wall. The door opened to reveal the house doctor, a short and stern looking man with black hair and a mustache. He ignored Cesar's presence and walked down the corridor in the direction of the drawing room.

Valencia emerged from the staff room soon after "On my authority, he will examine my father's body. Once he has done so, he will return to the staff room and await further instructions."

"It would only be a cursory examination of course," Cesar said. "A thorough post-mortem examination calls for surgical dissection."

"It will suffice for the time being" Valencia said bluntly. "Of more importance, I think, is what you plan to do now?"

"I was under the impression that you knew where I had to go?"

"And your impression is correct. Regardless, I must know more about what it is you are looking for, so that I may inform you of where you will most likely find it."

Cesar collected his thoughts and determined what his first order of business should be "I would benefit from learning more about your father and what his plans were for tonight. There's more to this situation then he was willing to reveal, and while I believe you have partial knowledge of it…"

"I do not know what you mean" she said hotly, Cesar ignored her.

"…I also believe that you knew less than your father did. Therefore, I would like to see his person effects if I could."

"What type of personal effects?"

"A journal, documents of his, items of that nature. Anything that has to the potential to produce important information."

"I see…The first place we would go then, would be my father's living quarters."

"He had his own bedroom at the hotel?"

"He and I had our own accommodations on the third floor. I will take you there."

They went to the nearest staircase and ascended to the third floor. The Decarlis' apartment was located at the end of a corridor at the far end of the hotel, the door to it was nondescript and no different from any other door, probably to make it appear unimportant.

Valencia produced a keyring with four keys on it "I've been coming to this hotel since I was a girl. Even before father purchased the property, we would always stay in this suite." She showed Cesar one of the keys "This key I have here is one of just two of its kind."

"Your father possessed the other one?"

"Obviously."

Her face fell as she inserted the key into the door.

Cesar noticed "What is it?"

"The door is already unlocked" she said stiffly.

Cesar took out his revolver and silently gestured for Valencia to step away from the door. With his weapon pointed in front of him, he opened the door and entered cautiously. The main feature of the Decarlis apartment was a spacious and ornately furnished living room with pale white walls and brown hardwood floors. On either side of the living room were two doors.

"Where do those doors lead?" Cesar asked.

"The one on the left is my father's room, the one on the right is mine" Valencia answered distantly, as she looked around to see if anything was out of place.

Cesar moved to inspect Alexander's room, he found this door unlocked as well and let himself in. The bedroom had brown decorative panel walls and red carpet. A door on the left-hand side led to an immaculate bathroom, he made sure nobody was in the bathroom before searching the bedroom. Apart from the four-poster bed, there was a roll-top desk, two dressers, a sofa, and a side-table. On top of the side table was a black and white photograph of an adult woman and a girl. Cesar soon realized the girl in the picture was a young Valencia Decarli, and therefore the woman was likely her mother. Cesar was greatly surprised by this, Valencia's mother was supposed to be a mystery, yet Alexander had a picture of her, so therefore it was not a mystery to him.

He then turned his attention to the roll-top desk. There were papers spread out on the desktop, but Cesar found very few of them to be important. The only paper of significance was a note written in ink.

Father

    I've done all that you requested that I do. Everyone at the Geraldine knows what's expected of them in this affair. Once you have arrived and are able to read this, the only roles left to play will be that of our own. I know you better than perhaps anyone in this life. I wish you would tell me more about what it is you hope to accomplish by bringing him and the others here. But I'm under no presumption that I can persuade you tell me more than what you have elected to tell me.

I feel as if a great event is about to happen, an event that will change everything, but I could not tell you what it is or be less confusing. Mother was the same way, she had premonitions that caused her duress, but knew little about them. Naturally you never had any patience for it.

I am distressed, but I am also hopeful. Being your daughter has more than prepared for me for all the distress that one can experience. The hope, I believe, is one other trait that comes from her.

Beloved Valencia

As Cesar finished reading the note, he quickly placed it back down on the desk and covered it with another piece of paper. He did not wish Valencia to know that he had seen it.

The roll top desk had many drawers which Cesar looked through one by one. The drawers were all either empty or filled with miscellaneous papers, all except one. The upper right-hand corner drawer had a false bottom, Cesar had seen enough drawers with false bottoms in his time to recognize them on sight.

He pulled the drawer out, set it on the desk, pried open the false bottom. Below the bottom was a grid-like arrangement of compartments, inside each compartment was a key. There was, however, one compartment with a key missing.

Cesar's inspection of the drawer was interrupted by footsteps behind him. He turned to see Valencia Decarli enter the room. In her hand was a gun.

Cesar pointed his LeMat revolver at her and expected her to do the same.

Instead she remained cool and looked at him sardonically. "Please" she said dryly "If I aspired to kill you I would not do so by gunning you down in my father's bedroom."

"Where did that gun come from?"

"From my room, where it's kept in my nightstand. It was a gift to my father from the fine people at *Waffenfabrik Bern*."

She offered the gun to Cesar with the muzzle pointing away from him, her way of showing that she meant no harm. Cesar took the gun and inspected it.

"This is a Swiss gun?"

"What else would it be?" she said pridefully as she took the gun back from him "What are you looking for in my father's desk?"

"Do you know about this?" Cesar said, pointing towards the drawer with the keys in it.

She blinked at the drawer "These keys belonged to my father, they are to various rooms in the hotel, including ones that are off limits to guests and most of the staff."

"One of them is missing."

"I beg your pardon?"

Cesar pointed towards the only compartment without a key. Valencia looked alarmed. "Where did it-"

"Do you know which room this key went to?"

"I…Yes…the hotel has a library. The library has a study which my father uses, the key to the study is the one missing."

Cesar smiled to himself "I know what might've happened."

"Well please tell me."

"You mentioned that your father was the only other with a key to this suite. Where would he have kept it?"

Valencia paused for thought before responding "On his person I'd imagine."

"Would he have had it on him when he died?"

Valencia's eyes widened in understanding.

"I believe the same man who killed your father took that key from his body, and then while you and I were waiting on the house doctor, he gained access to the suite, found this drawer, and took the key to this study you mentioned."

"Do you think it plausible that that person who took this key could be in that study right now?" Valencia suggested.

"If my hypothesis is correct, it is more than likely."

"Then we have no time to idle" she gestured for him to follow.

Cesar kept up with Valencia as she ran to the other side of the hotel and descended down a set of stairs, she eventually stopped at a set of wooden double doors on the first floor.

"This is the only way to the Geraldine's library. If this key thief of yours hasn't left yet, then he is somewhere behind these doors" Valencia explained, before discreetly opening one of the double doors and entering the library. Cesar entered the library with her and began searching the place.

Most of the library was below ground and only accessible by a spiral staircase. The library's upper floor consisted of a corridor that went along the edge of the library, a railing prevented anyone in this corridor from falling into the library's bottom floor.

Valencia led Cesar down this corridor to a door. The sound of someone rummaging around could be heard inside. Cesar leaned against the wall near the door and signaled for Valencia to do the same on the other side of the door. The two of them produced their weapons.

"Will you allow me to enter first?" Cesar said quietly.

"I'd prefer it" she said with a smirk.

Cesar positioned himself in front of the door and threw it open.

The study was in disarray, books had been thrown off their shelves and display cases had been smashed open. On one side of the study was a very large oak desk. Behind the desk, Sergei Melikov was in the process of upending and dumping out the contents of the desk drawers. When he saw Cesar, he gave no reaction and instinctively pulled a handgun from inside his suit jacket.

Cesar aimed and fired his revolver, the bullet narrowly missing Melikov's shoulder. The man instinctively ducked down behind the desk. Cesar ran towards the desk and vaulted across it just as

Melikov was standing back up to fire again. Cesar covered the distance between him and Melikov in time to grab the man's gun and point it towards the ceiling. Melikov fired a shot into the air as the two of them struggled for control of the weapon. Cesar's other hand still held his revolver which Melikov had also grabbed onto and was pointing towards the floor.

Neither of them paid any attention to Valencia as she flanked them from the right. In a few precise moves, she grabbed a letter opener from the desk and stabbed Melikov's left arm with it. Melikov snarled in pain and his grip on the LeMat revolver weakened. Cesar wrestled his revolver out of Melikov's hand and bashed him across the face with it. He tumbled to the ground and was subdued by Cesar and Valencia.

They used rope taken from the study's curtains to bound Melikov's hands to a wooden chair near the study's main window. It was not sufficient to hold anyone of considerable strength, but Melikov did not seem eager to escape from his predicament. He also seemed astonishingly tranquil for a man who had been stabbed in the arm and pistol whipped in the face. In the pockets of jacket, the two keys stolen from Decarli were found, the first from the man's corpse and the second from the man's bedroom. Also found was a bottle of poison.

"You said my father was poisoned?" Valencia said, doing an impressive job of compartmentalizing her rage "This proves it then doesn't it?"

"I would be very surprised if this wasn't the poison that killed your father" Cesar said as he examined at the bottle. "And since we found it on Melikov, that makes him the prime candidate for your father's killer."

"Why do you sound uncertain?" Valencia asked. "What is there to be uncertain of?"

Cesar thought of how strange it was for Valencia to be so calm in this situation; but disregarded it.

"There is something very off about all of this" he said solemnly. "Not just your father's murder, but the fact that he invited all of us here tonight for eight separate pieces of business. I for one would like Melikov to explain himself."

"There is nothing to explain" Melikov said in the wooden voice of a man who was soon scheduled to be executed. "I did what I was expected to do."

"Why did you kill my father!?" Valencia snapped suddenly, as if she had sensed Cesar wondering about her calmness.

"I did not."

"He was poisoned, and you have poison."

"It was given to me by the man who hired me."

"What man who hired you?" Cesar said sharply.

"You already know his name. He is here with us, we ate dinner with him. He used the poison to kill Decarli, and then he entrusted it to me."

Cesar paused for thought, his mind was racing "You are talking about one of the other six guests?"

"Yes"

"Which one?"

Melikov looked at Cesar with his dead eyes "I will not tell you."

Cesar figured he wouldn't. He stared into Melikov's green eyes but detected no weakness. Breaking him would be difficult.

"This man you're referring to…" Valencia said slowly, a meditative look on her face. "If he gave you the poison, then he must've surely been the one who killed my father?"

Melikov stared blankly at Valencia "I suppose there is no harm telling you now that Decarli is already dead, but you are correct, the man who hired me is also the man who killed Alexander Decarli."

Cesar had many questions "And what did you have to do with this? Did you know this was going to happen?"

Melikov nodded "I came here with the knowledge that the man

who hired me planned to kill Decarli. My primary reason for being here was to kill Decarli if my employer failed to do so."

"You said that you were hired by one of the guests here? But you were also invited by Decarli?"

"The man who hired me persuaded Decarli into inviting me. My name was added to the invitation at his insistence."

"Then you're not supposed to be here?"

"No, I am supposed to be here. Everyone here, including you Mondragon, was invited here by Decarli because there was a specific purpose in inviting them. His purpose for inviting me here was to ensure that the man who hired me would willingly come to tonight's events."

"Why? This man who hired you, whoever he is, what's so important about him that Decarli would invite you here just because he was asked to?"

"From what I understand, Decarli fully expected that the man who hired me would try to kill him. I would then guess that Decarli wanted to die at the hands of this man."

An uneasy silence filled the room.

Cesar was the one who broke the silence "What about this business he wanted to discuss with each of us? That story he told you about the Empress Maria Feodorovna and her associates?"

"A false narrative. Only he was to understand the real reason each person was here, therefore a fabricated reason was created for each person."

Cesar was having troubled processing all of this "Valencia, how much of this do you know about?"

Valencia was at a loss for words, and she looked upset about it "I suspected my father had his reasons for inviting you all here, and that the business he mentioned was not genuine, but I never suspected he was willingly arranging for himself to be murdered."

Cesar looked back to Melikov "You said that this man hired you? Why? What led him to hiring you as a potential killer?"

"Because I have a reputation for it."

"You're not really an accountant then?"

"I am many things."

Cesar only had a few more questions left "Why did you take the key to the study? What is it you were looking for in here?"

"Anything of relevance."

"And what would be of relevance to you?"

"Anything that would implicate the man who hired me or would reveal the reasons for his wanting Decarli dead. In addition to killing Decarli if he failed, I was also to assist him in recovering and destroying damaging information that could be used against him."

Cesar took his revolver out again "Tell me the identity of the man who hired you."

"No," Melikov said.

"I will kill you."

"Kill me."

Cesar lost his composure and raised his voice "You will-"

The sound of broken glass turned their attention to the window. They both saw a gloved hand sticking through a broken pane of glass, enclosed within the hand was an unidentified object. The hand opened, releasing the object, and then disappeared through the window. Cesar was aware that it was a grenade before it hit the floor.

Valencia soon realized that it was a grenade and ran for the door to the study. Cesar allowed himself one second to hesitate and then acted.

As Valencia fled from the study, Cesar immediately charged into her, grabbed her in his arms, and then flung himself over the railing into the library's bottom level. The two of them collided into one of the bookcases, which toppled over with them. The entire library was shaken by the detonation of the grenade.

Cesar and Valencia lay on the bookcase and took several seconds to catch their breath and allow what had just happened to fully dawn on them.

Valencia was on her feet first "Oh my God" she said in a shaken voice.

Cesar remained lying on top of the bookcase, allowing himself more time to recover.

"Are you alright?" Valencia said to Cesar, offering him her hand.

"Yes, I'm…fine."

She pulled him to his feet. "I don't mean to minimize what just happened, but was that bit of bravado on your part absolutely necessary?"

"We had to get as far away from that grenade as possible. They vary in their explosive range and are therefore unpredictable. There is also shrapnel, which will kill you if it ends up the right place…or the wrong place."

"You are knowledgeable about grenades" she said, almost in a complimentary manner.

"And a great many other things, few of which I enjoy being knowledgeable about."

"What of Mister Melikov then?"

"He is no more, as is your father's study I'm afraid."

"It seems the man who hired him had no more use for him" she said spitefully.

"Let's hope he does not come to the same conclusion about either of us."

The two of them ascended the spiral stairs to the top floor of the library and then quickly made their way to the double doors. Outside the library, they were greeted by the sight of Galopin running down the corridor towards them.

"I heard the gunshots!" he exclaimed. "What was that explosion?"

"One of the gunshots was my doing" Cesar immediately said. "Melikov pulled a weapon on me, I disarmed him."

"What? Melikov?" Galopin said, startled "Where is he?"
"He's dead, someone with a grenade saw to that."
Galopin gaped at Cesar.
"Mister Galopin, please…" Valencia said calmly "Come back to the drawing room with us, I will explain everything."

Chapter 6
A Pryce to Pay

Cesar was silent as they made their way back to the drawing room. Valencia contented herself with explaining to Galopin what had occurred in the library. Every question he had, she answered. She spoke till he was satisfied.

"I do not comprehend this" Galopin said acerbically "Two are dead, one by poison and another by grenade, and all this talk of absurd plots."

Cesar remained wary of Galopin. Despite appearing to be a truth-seeker and spectator, Cesar suspected that the French officer, like Melikov, knew much more than he was willing to admit. "Mister Galopin, Melikov said that Decarli invited everyone here to fulfill a specific purpose, and that the stated reasons for us being here were all a series of guises. I don't suppose you have some idea of your purpose?"

Galopin shook his head "I'm here because I was invited here. If there is a reason for my being here other than the reason I was given by Decarli, then I have no knowledge of it."

They entered the drawing room to find Dickerson and Rombauer standing and pacing anxiously. Biassiano was also there, he sat by himself and was still wearing the clothes he had arrived in. This prompted Cesar's suspicion, as less than an hour ago, Biassiano had declared his intention to retire for the night. Von Strichtenheimer and Pryce were nowhere to be seen.

Dickerson and Rombauer rushed up to Cesar, Valencia, and Galopin as they entered the drawing room.

"I demand to know what's going on in this godforsaken place?" Dickerson said stuffily.

"That noise, it was an explosion?" Rombauer said worriedly. "I've heard enough to know that it was one."

Galopin sighed "I regretfully announce to you all that Sergei Melikov has been murdered."

Dickerson and Rombauer were mortified, Biassiano looked over nonchalantly.

"Murdered?" Dickerson said breathlessly. "Another one? How? Was he poisoned as well?"

"Someone killed him with a grenade" Cesar said casually.

A shocked silence followed this revelation.

"A grenade" Dickerson said in an appalled voice, as if it was absurd. "What sort of..."

"Who killed him?" Biassiano asked, having gotten up from his seat and walked over.

"We did not see who did it" Cesar said.

"What do you mean you did not see them!?" Biassiano snapped. "Where did the grenade come from?"

"They were on the other side of a dark window, they broke part of the window and dropped the grenade in."

"This is insanity" Rombauer said quietly. "There is a murderer here and he has now killed two of us. We must leave this place at once, we are not safe here."

"Respectfully I disagree Ludwig" Dickerson said quickly "It is late at night and anyone who attempts to drive off or flee into the darkness will make themselves an easy prey for this madman."

"The Yankee is right, Doctor Rombauer" Biassiano concurred loudly. "It is better if you stay here and rely on the collective security of the group."

Rombauer looked between Dickerson and Biassiano, who were both looking at him with self-assured expressions "So that we may be easier victims?" he said indignantly.

Cesar spoke up "Doctor Rombauer, I don't think that you in particular are in any significant danger."

Everyone looked at Cesar "How do you mean?" Rombauer asked.

"Based on everything I've seen so far, tonight's events are not the work of a homicidal individual that desires to kill everyone here, but a plot specifically targeting Decarli. Melikov confessed to being part of this plot before he was disposed of by whoever his conspirator was."

"Did Melikov kill Decarli?" Dickerson asked.

"He claims that it was his conspirator and not him-"

"And you believe him?" Dickerson interrupted.

Cesar shot a glare at Dickerson "Somebody killed Sergei Melikov with a hand grenade, so I think it's incredibly unlikely that the man was a lone actor…"

The door to the drawing room opened behind Cesar, he turned to see Kenneth Pryce standing there with an unperturbed expression.

"Mister Pryce" Valencia said. "Where did you come from?

"I was upstairs in my room" Pryce said coolly. "What are we all talking about then?"

"Melikov is dead" Galopin said roughly.

Pryce narrowed his eyebrows "Is he now? And how did he die?"

"Miss Decarli and Mister Mondragon claim it was a grenade."

Pryce blinked, "That accounts for the noise I heard."

"That's what we 'claim,' is it not?" Valencia asked testily.

Galopin sighed and looked at her "I do not believe that you two are lying. It remains though, that you are the only two to have received this admission from Melikov. I was not there and therefore I cannot base it on anything other than what you've claimed."

"It does seem to be a curious change in methods" Pryce remarked. "They killed Decarli with poison and now they've killed Melikov with a grenade of all things."

"That is of course, assuming that the murderer of Alexander Decarli and Sergei Melikov are the same person" Cesar said confidently.

Galopin and Pryce both looked at Cesar "You would have us believe that there are two murderers here tonight?" Galopin asked.

"Major Galopin, I will not have you believe anything. I will only refer to what you and I both know: That we have all been brought to this hotel for reasons that're unclear to us, that our host has died from what appears to be poison, and that another guest was murdered right after he confessed to his involvement in a murder plot. Do you have a way to make sense of all of this?"

Galopin was silent for a long time. Cesar took this as a "No."

"What are we to do then?" Pryce wondered.

"I'd rather not leave this room" Dickerson said. "Things seem much safer in here."

"I agree with you *Herr* Dickerson" Rombauer said "*Herr* Mondragon is clearly able to address matters such as this. I think we should leave him to it."

"I do not give a damn what any of you do" Biassiano said.

Dickerson looked around at everyone "Well then…*Herr* Rombauer, how is your chess?"

"It's been a while, but it will return to me quickly."

The American and the German went off to one of the drawing room's chessboards.

"Where is von Strichtenheimer?" Galopin asked suddenly.

"He left" Biassiano said.

"Left where?"

"I do not know, I did not ask, and allow me to reiterate that I do not give a damn! I grow aggravated with your company, and now I am leaving!"

With that, Biassiano stormed out.

"Ever the charmer" Pryce said cheerfully.

"Pryce," Galopin said. "Did you see Von Strichtenheimer upstairs?"

"I did not."

Galopin turned to Cesar "Do you believe Von Strichtenheimer could be the grenadier that killed Melikov?"

"It is a possibility."

"An effort should be made to find him."

"Respectfully Major Galopin, I would not know where to look. My immediate order of business would be to examine Melikov's room at the hotel."

Galopin grunted "Yes of course, I will continue to allow you to conduct your own affairs. I shall look for Von Strichtenheimer on my own."

Galopin left.

"And what of you Mister Pryce?" Valencia asked. "

Pryce smiled goodheartedly and pointed towards Dickerson and Rombauer who were setting up a chessboard "I think I'll keep an eye on those chaps. Don't have much else to be doing."

"Very good. If you need me, Mister Mondragon and I will be looking around Mister Melikov's room."

Without another word, Valencia made her way out of the drawing room. Cesar exchanged a look with Pryce before hurrying after her.

They went up to the second floor in the corridor where Melikov's room was and unlocked it with a master key Valencia had in her possession. Cesar had expected there to be luggage or personal affects in the room, but there wasn't any to be seen.

"Did Melikov arrive at the hotel with any belongings?" Cesar asked Valencia.

"He had a case."

"Then it should be here somewhere. Unless he placed it elsewhere in the hotel."

They searched the room and found Melikov's case inside one of the dresser drawers. They then placed it on top of the dresser to open it. Inside the case were Melikov's clothes and a green leather-bound book.

"What do you suppose is in here?"

Valencia opened the book to see that it was filled with accounting information.

"I suppose he really was an accountant" Cesar said, "In addition to a hired killer."

"It's a useful trade" she said.

He looked at her.

"Accounting I mean" she clarified.

Cesar placed his hand on Melikov's clothes and felt something hard enclosed within the shirt, he unfolded the clothes and found that the object was a dagger within a scabbard.

"A dagger" Valencia observed, "Strange that he did not have it with him."

Cesar took the dagger out of the scabbard and examined it. The handle was black and possibly made of wood or ivory, there were miniscule bits of gold embedded within it. The image of a double-headed eagle was engraved in gold just beneath the hilt.

"I've seen a knife like this before."

Valencia was surprised "You have?"

"The two-headed eagle on the blade is particularly revealing. This is an Okhrana dagger."

"A what dagger?"

"Okhrana, the Russian secret police, or the former Russian secret police, I should say. They were formed by the Tsar near the end of the last century and were responsible for suppressing revolutionary activity in the Russian Empire…Given that the Russian Empire was overthrown by revolutionaries, I think it fair to say they were unsuccessful."

"How do you know so much about this?"

"I've encountered them before, former members of the Okhrana in exile across Europe. Many of them are quite old now and wait for death. Melikov was middle-aged, so he was probably among the last generation of them. The ones that still had fight in them would find new crusades. They'd continue to resist the communists who stole their motherland from them, they'd go to work for another nation's intelligence service, or they'd become hired agents. The ones I met had similar knives."

"Melikov must've been the latter than? A former secret policeman who became a hired agent? He has this dagger, and he said that he was hired by another guest. It would make a great deal of sense."

Cesar placed the dagger back in the scabbard, placed it back in the case, and closed it. "Be that as it may, it only tells us more about Melikov, and not about the man who hired him."

They left Melikov's room.

"What do you propose now?" Valencia asked Cesar as they walked down the corridor in the direction of the stairwell.

"The most pertinent thing to do is to find out the identity of the man who hired Melikov."

"And how would you go about that?"

"There's not much to go on, but it would be potentially useful if I were to ascertain whether or not Melikov's client and Melikov's killer are the same person."

"Yes, you mentioned that to the Major. Is it your present theory that there are two killers at hand or is it merely a possibility?"

"I think-"

Cesar was interrupted by Valencia, who pushed him into a dark alcove.

"What are-"

"Shh!" Valencia put her fingers to his lip. "Von Strichtenheimer" she whispered.

Valencia moved away so Cesar could peek out of the alcove. Sure enough, Von Strichtenheimer had emerged from an intersecting hallway and was now walking up the hallway they had just been in.

"What do you think he might be doing?" Valencia whispered.

Cesar watched Von Strichtenheimer disappear around a corner before deciding upon a course of action "We should follow him."

They shadowed Von Strichtenheimer as he made his way across the second floor. Cesar, who had shadowed people before and was quite proficient at it, guided Valencia through the process less she accidentally reveal the two of them.

Eventually Von Strichtenheimer went up a staircase to the third floor.

"What's on the third floor?" Cesar asked Valencia.

"You mean besides the apartment you saw? Primarily the hotel's more luxurious suites, and a room my father kept paintings in. My father was friends with Marc Chagall, did I ever mention that?"

Cesar wasn't listening and instead looked behind them to a darkly lit corridor that led off from the hallway they were currently in.

"Cesar?" Valencia said, looking at him.

She gave a frightened yelp as Cesar pulled out his revolver and aimed in the direction of the dark hallway. "You have five seconds to show yourself!" he said in an audible and clear voice.

"Alright! I'm coming out!" said another voice that was familiar.

Kenneth Pryce slowly revealed himself from the shadows he had been standing in, his hands out in front of him to show he meant no harm.

"Mister Pryce" Valencia said, only mildly surprised.

"Why are you following us?" Cesar asked.

"I'm not, I'm following Von Strichtenheimer" Pryce explained.

"Why?"

"For the same reason you are I imagine, you are suspicious of him."

"Why did you not make yourself known?"

"Alerting you would've risked alerting Von Strichtenheimer, and I anticipated that you would not rush to welcome my presence."

"You anticipated correctly" Cesar said in an unfriendly voice.

"Mister Mondragon please, you are right to be suspicious of me, but I assure you I have no malevolent intentions towards you."

Cesar scoffed "In my experience, those with malevolent intentions do not often inform others of them."

Pryce hung his head "Yes, you're quite right about that." He quickly perked up again "I'll have to prove it to you then. I shall be returning to my room at the hotel where I will remain for the next hour or so. When you are ready, come find me there and I will explain certain things to you."

"Explain to me now."

"I think it's been made clear that we do not know who may be listening. I swear on any shred of dignity I have, I will explain all that I can once I am in the relative security of my room."

"I do not know where your room is."

"I know where Mister Pryce is staying" Valencia said. "I will show you Cesar, and I'll even accompany you."

"That's fine" Pryce said agreeably "What I can explain to you, I can also explain to her."

Cesar scrutinized Pryce "I will consider it."

"That's all I ask… Am I free to leave?"

Cesar gestured for Pryce to leave with his revolver. He waited until he was sure Pryce was gone before speaking "Do you see that he dropped something?"

"Excuse me?"

Cesar knelt down and picked up a small object from the floor, it was a pin with a ring attached at one end of it. He handed it to Valencia.

"I saw it fall out of Pryce's coat, but I did not alert either him or you to it."

She inspected it "But…What is it?"

"I think it's the pin to a hand grenade."

Valencia looked at Cesar. "The pin to a..." she allowed herself a moment to realize what Cesar was saying, "Do you mean that Pryce was the one we encountered in the library? The one who killed Melikov and may've been trying to kill us as well?"

"He was absent from the drawing room when we arrived there with Galopin, and when he did arrive, he vaguely claimed to be upstairs. Now he's dropped an item that resembles a hand grenade pin. All these factors mean he is the most likely candidate for whoever it was outside the library window."

"But…this does not necessarily mean that Pryce is also the man Melikov spoke of? The one who hired him and killed my father?"

"It doesn't necessarily mean he's not that man either. Still, I am not at the point where I can make such postulations. Let us find where Von Strichtenheimer went, and then we will see what Pryce has to offer."

Cesar and Valencia went up to the third floor in search of Von Strichtenheimer, but it was not clear where he went.

"Where did he go?" Cesar wondered.

"Perhaps we should split up?" Valencia suggested.

"Are you sure that's a good idea?"

She held up her revolver "Have I not demonstrated that I can take care of myself?"

"My apologies…Yes of course, we shall search the floor separately."

Cesar went down the hall while Valencia went in the opposite direction. The doors to nearly all the rooms on the third floor were locked. This either meant that Von Strichtenheimer had access to a key and locked himself behind one of these doors, or that he was still prowling these halls somewhere.

Cesar stopped at a corner when he heard voices, he looked around to see Von Strichtenheimer talking to Biassiano. The conversation soon became an argument, and that argument soon became a violent altercation with each other. As the two men struggled, Cesar took the opportunity to dart behind a suit of armor that was on display in the hall.

Biassiano eventually won the scrap and pinned Von Strichtenheimer against a wall, the Italian fascist pulled out a dagger and pointed it against the Austrian nobleman's face. Cesar put his hand on his revolver, ready to intervene if the situation became dire. Fortunately for Von Strichtenheimer, Biassiano seemed content to hold the knife against his face.

"Are you going to scream?" Biassiano asked in a taunting voice.

"You flatter yourself!" Von Strichtenheimer snapped, his voice was firm and resolute. Cesar recognized it as the voice of someone who was unafraid to die.

"Calm yourself *Austriaco*, I only wish to ask you a question."

"How to make a proper noose?"

"Most amusing, but no. I'd like to know what you are doing here?"

"You will have to be more specific."

"Why did Decarli invite you to this hotel? And answer wisely because we are all aware that what he told us was fiction. He did not invite you here because Hitler annexed your country, nor did he invite me because of artifacts stolen from my country. Now tell me the real reason you're here."

"You first Mister Blackshirt. Why are you at the Hotel Geraldine?"

"I came here for one man."

"Which one man?"

"I would not tell you."

Von Strichtenheimer laughed, impressive since there was a knife against his face "I too, came here for one man."

"The same one as I?"

"If you will not tell me, then I shall not tell you."

"You presume you and I are equals?" Biassiano said unpleasantly.

"Oh, to the contrary."

Biassiano saw that Von Strichtenheimer would not be intimidated and punched the man in the stomach.

"It ultimately matters not to me why you are here, so long as you do not prove an interloper to me."

"I cannot prove an interloper if I do not know why you're here" Von Strichtenheimer strained to say, his hand on his stomach where Biassiano punched him.

Biassiano looked at him with contempt "You are a remnant of a past age. An idle nobility that reaps the rewards of empire. The new empires are already being built and they belong to those who have the will and the strength to build them. If you do not believe me, then look to your Austria. Not only it is no longer an empire, but now because of the Anschluss it is no longer a country. A generation from now, Italia and Germania will have claimed their rightful place as the dominant powers of Europe, and the once mighty Austro-Hungarian Empire will be but a memory."

"The Nazis will not share their power with Italy. They ally with you out of necessity. Once Britain, France, and the Bolsheviks have been pulverized, they will set their sights south of the alps."

"One war at a time, eh?" Biassiano quipped.

He kicked Von Strichtenheimer once more and then marched down the hall away from him. He passed Cesar in his hiding spot as he marched. As Cesar watched him go by, he thought about how he could've pulled out his revolver and shot the man in the head. It was a pleasurable thought, but ultimately it was just a thought.

Once Biassiano was gone, Cesar looked back to Von Strichtenheimer to see the man had gotten to his feet. His face was not visible to Cesar, but the sounds of breathing he was making made it clear how apoplectic he was. He marched away, opposite from the direction Biassiano had gone, and disappeared around a corner.

Cesar emerged from his hiding place and quickly made his way to the spot where Von Strichtenheimer was last seen. To Cesar's great surprise, the corridor ended in a dead end, and Von Strichtenheimer was nowhere to be seen.

He retraced his steps back to the corridor where he and Valencia had split up in. A few minutes of waiting went by before Valencia showed up herself.

"I saw Biassiano" she said to Cesar.

"I saw him too, him and Von Strichtenheimer."

He explained to her the encounter he had witnessed and how Von Strichtenheimer had vanished through a solid wall.

"I'm not sure who to be more suspicious of" Valencia mused. "Biassiano or Von Strichtenheimer."

"With Biassiano, it's difficult to distinguish between suspicious behavior and him just being his awful self. Von Strichtenheimer however, somehow found a way to walk through walls."

"Are you certain he went down that corridor?"

"There weren't many places to go, so yes, I'm certain of it."

"Father always did say this hotel had a habit of bringing out the madness in people."

Cesar looked at his pocket watch. "Pryce said he'd been in his room for an hour, I propose we go and see him now."

They went back down the stairs to the second floor and to the front of the hotel near where Pryce's room was. On the way there, they ran into the doctor that Valencia had sent to examine her father's body.

"Miss Decarli, I have been looking for you."

"Oh, my word, Doctor Gounelle. I'm so sorry, I almost forgot about you."

"I did as you asked and examined your father. I am most afraid that you were correct, he does appear to have been poisoned. But I am unable to tell what type of poison it was."

Valencia reached into her pocket and pulled out the bottle of poison they had took from Melikov. "I think you will find that it was this poison that killed him."

Doctor Gounelle peered at the bottle of poison Valencia held, and then cast a hurried look at Cesar. "Miss Decarli, will you please come with me to my office? I have books of poison there, and I feel that it would be best if you and I were to identify this poison together."

"Can it not wait?"

"I believe we should do it as soon as possible."

Valencia sighed and looked at Cesar "Shall I trust you to meet with Pryce on your own?"

"I think I will manage. Thank you, Valencia."

Valencia handed Cesar a ring of four keys "The silver one is the master key for most rooms at the hotel. Should Pryce have locked his door, you can feel free to let yourself in."

Valencia and Doctor Gounelle went to the hotel's central staircase while Cesar followed her directions to Pryce's room.

Bearing in mind that Pryce was most likely the man who almost killed him with a grenade, he kept his right hand near the revolver in his coat. With his left hand, he knocked on the door and waited for Pryce's answer, but no answer came. He knocked once more "Mister Pryce?"

No answer came.

Cesar checked to see if the door was locked and found that it was, just as Valencia had suggested. He took out Valencia's master key and entered Pryce's room. He was unprepared for what he found.

Kenneth Pryce lay face first on the floor of his room, his body bore the signs of more than a dozen stab wounds. He was unmistakably dead.

Chapter 7
Behind the Walls, Under the Floors

As Cesar stared down at Kenneth Pryce's corpse, he was aware of how he felt no shock or revulsion. There was perhaps a time in his past where he would've been aghast by the sight of a person who had been stabbed to death, but through the years Cesar had become accustomed to human awfulness and could scarcely remember such an innocent time.

Instead the sight of Pryce's corpse invoked a feeling of aggravation, the aggravation of having been inconvenienced. Three murders meant three times during the night that he had been deprived of the chance to learn more of the circumstances that had brought him to this hotel. Alexander Decarli had been poisoned before Cesar had the opportunity to have a one-on-one meeting with him, Sergei Melikov had been blown up with a grenade when there was still information for Cesar to obtain from him, and now Kenneth Pryce, who was willing to share with Cesar everything he knew about the events that were taking place at the Hotel Geraldine, lay dead on the floor of his room.

Cesar leaned into the hall to make sure there was nobody in the vicinity and then entered the room, closing and locking the door behind him. He pulled out his revolver and turned to address the room as if it were full of people "If the one who did this is still in the room, or at the very least can hear my voice, know that I have no intention of turning you over to any authorities. You will die here tonight."

He searched the bathroom, the wardrobe, and under the bed,

but there was no other living person in the room. The killer was gone, but Pryce's blood was still wet, which meant it had to have happened recently.

Pryce's belongings were spread out across the bed, the man's empty suitcase and photography bag lay discarded on the floor. Cesar remembered how Melikov had been looking for nebulous items of an incriminating nature and wondered if whoever was responsible for killing Pryce was looking for similar nebulous items in the man's luggage.

Cesar searched through Pryce's belongings, but all there was to find were the man's clothes, a few books for light reading, and photography equipment. Once he determined there were no items in the room, he moved on to the unpleasant task of searching Pryce's dead person. In the pockets of Pryce's jacket, Cesar found the key to his room, a match book, and a book. The book was "Statism and Anarchy" by Mikhail Bakunin. He opened the book to find a photograph wedged between the front cover and the first page.

The photograph was of two men, who judging by their military fatigues, were soldiers of some sort. They were holding either side of a flag and displaying it for the camera. The man on the left had his right hand raised in a clenched fist salute and wore a look of defiant pride. The man on the right seemed more at ease and just looked earnestly towards the camera. Neither man was smiling. Since the photograph was in black and white, Cesar was unable to tell what type of flag it was or when or where this picture was taken. Fortunately, the clenched fist salute made it obvious to Cesar when and where this photograph was taken.

The raised fist in the air as symbol of revolution and resistance was associated with the Republican forces of the Spanish Civil War, that meant these men were more than likely soldiers fighting for the Republicans. The war had begun three years ago after a military coup against Spain's democratic government. However, the coup failed to consolidate control of Spain and the nation was fractured between two factions: There were the Republicans, who were an alliance of left-wing political groups and military forces loyal to the former government; and then there were the Nationalists, an alliance of right-wing political groups and the military forces who had supported the coup. The war had ended last Spring with the Nationalists having seized control of most of Spain, which made them the apparent victors. What was left of the Republicans had either left Spain or gone into hiding. This was the extent of everything Cesar knew about the conflict.

Kenneth Pryce had been a photographer and was therefore the one who probably took this photo, this meant that he was present in Spain when the war took place and was in the company of the Republican forces. What was more, there was a great possibility that Pryce fought in the war himself as a foreign volunteer for the Republicans. It made sense given that Pryce was a socialist. The Republicans had enjoyed the support of thousands of foreign volunteers, including many socialists, communists, and anarchists. They saw the Spanish Civil War not simply as a national conflict, but as an ideological conflict. To them the war represented a struggle between the forces of the old world; a world that belonged to kings, priests, and landowners, and the forces of a new world that was slowly emerging; a world that would belong to the masses.

Cesar was about to place the photo back in the journal when he noticed something about it, something he should've realized sooner, and likely would've if had not been so preoccupied with the three murders that had taken place tonight.

One of the men in the photo, the one who's fist wasn't in the air, he was one of the men who was here tonight at the Hotel Geraldine: It was Dieudonne Galopin. There was no mistaking the face, even his eyes still radiated strength and conviction through the photograph. None of the research Cesar had conducted on Galopin indicated that he had fought for the Republicans in the Spanish Civil War. It was well known that Galopin had supported the Republican cause and that he had urged the French government to drop the pretense of neutrality and take action to prevent the loss of Spain to Fascism. But if this photograph was genuine, then it meant that he had done much more than advocate for the Republicans, he had acted himself, either of his own unsanctioned volition, or as part of a special operation backed by the French government.

What was of greater significance to Cesar, was that if Kenneth Pryce had indeed taken this photograph, then it meant that he and Galopin had encountered each other during the Spanish Civil War. Two of the guests Alexander Decarli had invited to the Hotel Geraldine, had once stood next to each to other on a battlefield in Spain, and one of them had taken another's photograph.

Cesar's mind was filled with possibilities. Was the Spanish Civil War at the center of this somehow? Did Alexander Decarli have an agenda rooted in that conflict? It would be unsurprising given the man's reputation. Decarli thought nothing of profiting from the Great War or affiliating with both sides of the conflicts in Ireland and Russia. Why would the war in Spain be any different?

Such a theory still didn't explain why Cesar was there. He had nothing to do with the war. The last time he had been in Spain was years ago, before the war even started. He avoided war torn countries if he could. He knew from his own experiences that war made people more terrible and unpredictable than they already were.

Cesar placed Pryce's journal with the dead man's other belongings but kept the photograph for himself. There was one other question to consider, and that was how Pryce's killer had gained entry to the room. Pryce had locked himself into the room and Cesar had gained entry with Valencia's master key. Cesar had originally speculated that Pryce had let his killer in, and that the killer had taken Pryce's key and locked the room with it. But finding Pryce's key on his person did away with that idea.

There was also the possibility that the killer had their hands on a master key similar to the one Valencia had. If Valencia had such a key, then her father Alexander would've also had one. When Melikov stole the key to the Decarlis' suite, perhaps he also stole Decarli's master key as well? Before his death in the study of the library, he would've given the key to the man he mentioned, the one who was responsible for hiring him and ensuring his invitation to the Hotel Geraldine. That man would've then used the master key to kill Pryce in his own room and lock the door when he left.

There was another possibility that Cesar could not discount, and that was that the killer had gained access to Pryce's room without using the door. It was somewhat far-fetched, but Cesar had seen such a thing before: People accessing places they shouldn't have been able to; using windows, fireplaces, squeezing themselves through holes and crevices, and even hidden passageways. There were no windows or fireplaces in the room, nor did there appear to be a hole or crevice anywhere in the room, that just left the possibility of a hidden door or passageway.

Cesar began to inspect the room more closely. Like his room, it was a four-poster bedroom, but rather than colors of purple and white, its décor emphasized the colors of green and grey. Aside from the bed, there was a dresser, a wardrobe, a desk, and an assortment of chairs and tables. There was also, curiously enough, a painting. This was of note to Cesar because he had recalled seeing a similar painting in his and Melikov's rooms. It was a painting of a pastoral scene, and barely visible in part of the painting was what looked to be a distant man-made structure, a tower or castle of some kind.

He went over to the painting and to examine it more closely. As he looked at it, it only then occurred to him how out of place it seemed in the room. He carefully placed both hands on the painting and removed it from the wall. On the wall behind the painting was a hole, and within that hole was a lever. Cesar stared at the lever in the wall for a long moment, unsure of if it was wise for him to pull it. He quickly decided it was a risk he wanted to task and pulled the lever

The sound of a door opening directed Cesar's attention to the wardrobe. Feeling excitement that did not come often to him, he put the painting back on the wall and positioned himself in front of the wardrobe. He did not know what to expect and pulled out his LeMat revolver once more. With the gun pointed in front of him, he opened the door to the wardrobe. The back of the wardrobe had a door and it revealed a dark passageway that ran behind the room and several other rooms.

Cesar entered the passageway and began to slowly make his way towards wherever it went. He soon discovered that it didn't necessarily lead to any single location. He found doors that he realized led to other rooms in the hotel. He spent a few minutes wandering around, surprised at the extensiveness of this passageway system. Why had this hotel been designed like this? He'd been to buildings that had been designed to keep secrets. Judging by the age of the hotel, it had been built during a time of conflict and uncertainty.

Eventually he heard distant voices and thought it appropriate to make his way in their direction. He was able to tell that he was getting closer because the voices were steadily getting more audible. His pursuit led him to a dead end. As he was irately pondering why the tunnels would have dead ends, the voices spoke again.

"What does *Zwischenzug* mean in English?"

"It means 'intermediate move.'"

He recognized the voices, they belonged to Dickerson and Rombauer. And they must've been right on the other side of one of the stone walls of the tunnel. The two of them had scarcely left the drawing room since Decarli died, if they had even left at all. This meant the drawing room was likely on the other side of one of these walls.

Cesar assumed there was a purpose to this dead end and sought to take a closer look, he pulled a lighter out of his coat. He disliked tobacco, but the usefulness of a lighter meant he always had one concealed on him.

The flame from the lighter was bright enough to reveal a slot in the wall in front of him. It was at eye level and resembled the type of eye slots you put on doors, which left little ambiguity as to what it was for.

He opened the slot, and sure enough there were eyeholes. The light from outside the tunnels created two beams of light that shined on his face. He was about to look through the eyeholes, but the thought that they might be a trap for some unfortunate tunnel trespasser made him hesitate. He inspected the eyeholes, concluded it was probably safe, and then carefully looked through them.

Cesar was given a bird's eyes view of part of the drawing room. It was the part near the fireplace, where Valencia had first gathered the guests at the beginning of the night. Dickerson and Rombauer were both sitting on either side of a chess table and playing a friendly game, they hadn't the faintest idea Cesar was looking down at them.

"I know you aren't trying to win," Dickerson asserted. "At least not fully."

"I'm sure I don't know what you're speaking of," Rombauer mumbled.

"I'm not a stupid or uneducated man, but I'm also no renowned mind like you. If you so desired, you could've quickly tilted the odds in your favor."

Rombauer chortled and waved his hand dismissively "Please sir, your flattery isn't needed. I'm advanced in a few fields, it is true. But chess isn't one of my fields."

"I've known many advanced men and women myself. Even with what they're not good at, they're still better than the rest of us."

The sound of one of the drawing room doors opening caused Dickerson and Rombauer to temporarily glance away from their game. They seemed to be looking at whoever had just entered the room, Cesar couldn't see who it was as he didn't have a full view of the drawing room.

"Hello there," Dickerson said to the unidentified person. He received no response.

The sound of footsteps could be heard. Von Strichtenheimer wandered into Cesar's view, he walked over to a comfortable looking chair and sat down at it. He paid no attention to Dickerson or Rombauer and wore a distant look on his face. It was as if he was in the room, but his mind was elsewhere.

"Sir, are you troubled?" Dickerson asked.

This stirred something in Von Strichtenheimer, he blinked in astonishment and shot a look at the American "Why would I be? Has something troubling occurred?" he asked wryly.

Dickerson looked a bit surprised as he was confronted with the inanity of his question, but he soon smiled and nodded in a good-natured sort of way "Yes, of course…A stupid question. I've been known for them…But I trust you'll take my word when I profess not that often."

Dickerson's banter wasn't reciprocated by Von Strichtenheimer, who looked obstinately serious. "Surely this isn't the best time to play chess?" he asked, sounding a bit more affable than before.

"Do you have preferable means to pass the time when you're in a strange place, your host is dead, and his killer is lurking about somewhere?"

"And how do you know the man you're playing with is not his killer?"

Dickerson glanced at the grandfatherly Rombauer "I like my chances."

Cesar once again heard the sound of the drawing room doors opening.

"Ah! Von Strichtenheimer!" a French accent declared jubilantly, making it more than clear to Cesar who this person was.

Von Strichtenheimer frowned in the direction of Galopin as he approached. "Uh…Yes, what it is?"

Galopin walked into view "I have been looking for you, where have you been?"

"Why have you been looking for me?" Von Strichtenheimer asked, looking displeased.

"Do you know the Russian is dead?"

This was news to Von Strichtenheimer "What?" he exclaimed. "Melikov died? How?"

"You didn't hear it?" Rombauer asked.

"Hear what?"

"The grenade."

Von Strichtenheimer stared at Rombauer in disbelief.

"Decarli's daughter and Mondragon had found him somewhere where he should not have been. They were questioning him, and someone threw a grenade through a window."

Galopin, Dickerson, and Rombauer were all silent as Von Strichtenheimer took in this information.

"Why would…" Von Strichtenheimer began to ask, but the look on his face indicated he knew it was a futile question.

"We don't know. It's but another one of the night's mysteries."

Von Strichtenheimer gently shook his head and stood up from his chair "And are we any closer to solving any of them?"

"Ask Mondragon if you see him," Dickerson suggested. "He and Miss Decarli are around here somewhere."

"I shall be looking for them next," Galopin said. He gave Von Strichtenheimer, Dickerson and Rombauer a quick nod each, an undecipherable look on his warlike face. "Look after yourselves gentlemen."

Galopin took his leave.

"Would you like to play next?" Rombauer proposed to Von Strichtenheimer.

"No thank you, I wish to go outside. The night air always helps me think."

"Do be careful sir," Dickerson warned. "I shouldn't hope to find out you have also died."

"I'm always careful," Von Strichtenheimer said over his shoulder as he walked off.

Cesar had seen all he needed to and closed the eye slot. He went back to navigating the tunnels, occasionally hearing other voices in the distance. A few minutes of walking led him to what looked like a narrow set of darkly lit stairs. He descended the stairs, careful not to misstep. The stairs ended at a door, which was naturally locked.

He cursed the lock door and dreaded having to go back up the dark stairs, but then he remembered Valencia's words that the master key unlocked most doors at the Hotel Geraldine. He took out the key ring and put the master key into the lock, but it was not a match. He wanted to give up, but he could sense that he was on the verge of making an incredible discovery. He tried the other three keys on the key ring and was elated when the second one he tried unlocked the mysterious door.

The subterranean room Cesar entered was dimly lit and had the appearance of being older than any other room he had seen at the hotel. The walls and floor were made of stone, the only source of illumination was a dozen candles that gave the entire room a bluish appearance. Most of the room was barren aside from the candleholders and the few pieces of furniture it had. In the center of room was a circular table and two red armchairs. At the far end of the room a large rectangular table that was cluttered with numerous items, not far from the table was great old decorative storage chest. There was also a stove, it was attached to a chimney to allow for ventilation. And next to the stove there was a station for making tea.

Cesar went over to the large rectangular table. There was so much to see that Cesar was unsure of where to look first. Perhaps most prominent was a large map of Europe with garment buttons placed at specific locations on it. Cesar saw that there were eight of these buttons, just as there were eight guests had been invited to the Hotel Geraldine. It soon became clear that each button represented a different guest and their location reflected their country of residence.

Cesar's button was the color white and was in England, where his house in Oxford was. Likewise, Felix Von Strichtenheimer's button was black and was in the Netherlands, Sergei Melikov's button was red and was in Denmark, Ludwig Rombauer's button was pink and was in Sweden, and Pietro Biassiano's button was yellow was in Italy.

Galopin and Pryce's buttons, which were the colors of blue and green, were in different parts of France. Galopin in Paris and Pryce down near the Spanish border. Francis Edmund Dickerson's button, which was brown, was at the far-left end of the map, in the Atlantic Ocean, this was obviously meant to indicate he lived in the United States.

In addition to the garment buttons, there was a single glass chess piece located on Luxembourg where they presently were, a Queen piece. He ceaselessly analyzed this map, hoping in vain to find some hidden information on it.

Cesar tore his eyes away from the map to look at the other items on the table. There was a set of floorplans of the Hotel Geraldine, which appeared to include all its' secret rooms and passageway. He also saw that each of the guests had their names written on the rooms they had been assigned. He did not hesitate to grab them, rolled them up, and place them inside his coat.

The next item was a wooden box which contained three knives and two pistols, a small pocket revolver and an American M1911 pistol. Cesar grabbed the pistol and tucked it into the back of his pants. With three dead bodies in this hotel, he didn't mind having another weapon.

There was an unframed photograph that sat on the table. It was a formal picture of a family of three, a man, a woman, and a young girl. The man was clearly Alexander Decarli when he had been twenty years younger, the woman was the same one Cesar had seen upstairs in Alexander's bedroom, and the young girl was obviously Valencia. Cesar recognized the room the picture was taken in as the drawing room of the Hotel Geraldine. Written in cursive on the back of the photograph was "All roads lead to Rome…All roads lead home."

The last thing to look at was a written message. It was not unlike the message Cesar had encountered earlier, the one Valencia had written to her father. But to Cesar's surprise, this one was written to Valencia by her father.

Beloved Valencia

Once again, I am pleased that you have done everything I have needed you to do. It is simply one of the many times in this life that you have pleased me with your intelligence and reliability.

You expressed your wish for me to tell you more about why I've brought him and the others here, and I respect that wish. Sadly, I insist that I not tell you until the day before the events we have planned are to take place. I promise that by the time we are ready to begin at the Geraldine, you will know all that I do, including the reason that he must be here.

I also want you to know that you and your mother are the greatest thing that ever happened to me. I dread what I would be and what the world would be like, had I not met her and had the two of us not created you. My only regret is that I won't be here to see how

*your story ends, but I take great comfort knowing you will be here
to see how mine does.*

*Your father, and the one who you know better than anyone else
in this life, Alexander*

Cesar carefully folded this letter and placed it up his sleeve. He
had seen enough and now it was time for him to go. But before he
left, he wanted to make sure he knew where he was going. He still
wanted to search Biassiano's room, so he unfolded the map to the
Hotel and found out how to access the Italian's room from where
he was.

After he had finished searching the room, he decided that the
next order of business would be to inform someone of Pryce's
demise, that and confront Valencia Decarli. He was adamant that
she eventually tell him all that she knew.

An Event in Luxembourg

ACT

III

Chapter 8
The Tipping Point

Cesar peaked through Biassiano's wardrobe to make sure the man wasn't in his room. He stepped out onto the room's carpet and soundlessly closed the door to the wardrobe. Before he confronted Valencia about what he found downstairs, he had another room to search.

Cesar peaked through Biassiano's wardrobe to make sure the man wasn't in his room. He stepped out onto the room's carpet and soundlessly closed the door to the wardrobe. Before he confronted Valencia about what he found downstairs, he had another room to search.

He found Biassiano's case under the bed and set it down on the top of the bed. The case had a four-digit combination locked on it, yet for some reason Biassiano had left it unlocked. When he opened the case, he found that it held Biassiano's clothes and travel documents. The only other item was a medal, which Cesar inspected.

Inscribed on the edges of the medal was *"Marcia sv Roma. 27 Ottobre – 1 Novembre 1922."* This medal was for Biassiano's participation in the March on Rome nearly seventeen years prior. A good luck charm he carried with him it seemed.

Cesar closed the case, but as he did so he discovered there wasn't any clear way for him to lock it. This made no sense, why would there be a combination lock on the case if it couldn't be locked?

Wait...

Feeling a sense of excitement, he placed the year "1922" into the combination lock. The case made a clicking sound that signaled he had done something successfully. Cesar opened the case again and saw that a small hidden compartment on its roof had opened up, In the compartment was a folded-up piece of paper.

Cesar quickly looked at the door to the room, the thought of Biassiano entering at any moment kept him alert. He turned back to the case and retrieved the paper from it. He was concerned about ripping the paper in his excitement, so he unfolded it with more caution than perhaps necessary.

NAME: Francis Edmund Dickerson

PERSONAL INFORMATION: Born June 23, 1885 in Ravenna, Ohio.

Graduated from Northwestern University in 1907.

Worked as middle-management for his family's company Reynolds-Dickerson Metals from 1907 to 1912. Afterwards he would work as a treasurer for numerous companies in the Cleveland/Pittsburg area.

In 1912, he joined a philanthropic group that raised money for the families of victims of the RMS Titanic disaster. Through this group, he made numerous acquaintances and was able to procure a reputation as an "unofficial ambassador for worthy causes."

FAMILY INFORMATION: Father is Elias Andrew Dickerson. Mother is Imelda Dickerson (nee Kendrick.) Named after his grandfathers, Edmund Ralph Dickerson and Francis Xavier Kendrick. Wife is Millicent "Millie" Wexford-Madison.

Son is Francis Edmund Dickerson II. Daughter is Eileen Somerville (nee Dickerson.)

The Dickerson family became prominent in Ohio politics during the American Civil War and would later go on to make a fortune from Copper mining in Arizona.

His maternal family, the Kendricks are Maryland Catholics who've produced a noticeable number of theologians, academics, and merchants.

POLITICAL INFORMATION: Dickerson is part of the American Republican Party; yet is also cordial with many prominent figures in the American Democratic Party. He has personally met the current American President Franklin Delano Roosevelt, as well as previous Presidents Herbert Hoover, Calvin Coolidge, and William Howard Taft.

Several members of the Dickerson Family have enjoyed professional and personal connections with American Presidents dating as far back as President Ulysses S. Grant.

KNOWN ACTIVITIES: Beginning in 1935, Dickerson began to make foreign trips to Canada, England, and France. Always for formal events held at estate houses or diplomatic missions.

These trips appear to be correlated with the increase in tensions between the European powers.

ALLEGIANCES: Dickerson is a private citizen and officially holds no position in the American government. He's known to give anodyne and diplomatic answers when asked about world affairs. Otherwise, there is no indication he's anything more or less than a loyal subject of Anglo-American society.

RECOMMENDED ACTIONS: The possibility of Dickerson being an asset of his government cannot be definitively proven, but also cannot be discounted. He mustn't be allowed to undermine any effort that is of importance to Italian civilization or the National Fascist Party. If the opportunity presents itself, he should be eliminated with the utmost discretion.

It was of little mystery to Cesar what he was reading, this was a dossier on Dickerson. It was also an Italian intelligence document, which Cesar knew because he had seen such documents before. Why did Biassiano have this? Was Dickerson here tonight on behalf of American intelligence? And what of Biassiano? Was he here for Dickerson? Were they both here for something else?

Each question only led to more questions.

He hastily searched Biassiano's room for anything else that could prove useful; but turned up nothing. He was about to leave before the Italian fascist turned up, but then decided it was necessary to take Dickerson's dossier with him and show it to the American the next time he encountered him.

Now back outside in the hotel's corridors, Cesar set out to find Valencia Decarli. She had last gone to the staff room with the hotel's doctor, so that was where he was headed. The process of finding his way there was a little more difficult than he expected. The labyrinthian hotel was centuries old, and certain darkly lit corridors went without electricity. It would've been too dark to see his new map, so he merely made his way in what seemed like the right direction.

Cesar was on the first floor and had found a corridor with better lighting, which was a reassuring sign. The last thing he was expecting was for someone to sneak up behind him.

"And what might you be up to?" said a voice.

Cesar spun around, his hand reaching for his revolver as he did so.

Dieudonne Galopin stood imposingly before him. Cesar did not know if the French officer had been following him like Pryce had, or if he had happened to come from a nearby door or hallway.

"You should not startle me like that" Cesar spat at him.

"Ha!" Galopin guffawed, "Consider yourself fortunate."

Cesar looked at him questioningly.

"I've not had the luxury of being 'startled' since the Battle of Verdun" Galopin explained, unsmiling. "If you had also been there, then you too would not be jarred by much of anything afterwards."

Galopin did not say anything else and just stared severely at Cesar, his thoughts probably preoccupied with Verdun.

"I…" Cesar said, hesitating briefly, "I have bad news for you."

Galopin eyed him mistrustfully "What would that be?"

"Not out here in the hall. We should find a room to speak in."

To Cesar's surprise, Galopin didn't object to this and instead gestured towards the nearest door.

The room they found themselves in appeared to be a dusty lounge room. Cesar found a light switch and closed the door, Galopin crossed his arms and inclined his head towards Cesar, as if commanding him to speak.

"Kenneth Pryce has died."

Galopin looked amused "What?"

"I found him stabbed to death in his hotel room."

The two of them stared at each other, Cesar remained steadfastly serious, Galopin's look of amusement changed to one of disbelief "You are serious, aren't you?"

"Have I said or done anything tonight…" Cesar said "that would make you think I'd be unserious about this?"

Cesar saw in Galopin's face an emotion he had not seen him display before, and it was grief. "I do not…How is it that…" he tried to speak but words failed him.

"What was he to you?" Cesar asked.

Galopin avoided looking Cesar in the eyes "I do not understand the question" he said unconvincingly.

As a military man who wore his heart on his sleeve, Galopin was not skilled in deception. Cesar did not seek to be cruel to him, and simply produced Pryce's photograph of him.

Galopin stared at the photograph as Cesar showed it to him. It took a moment for him to realize he was looking at a photograph of himself, a thunderstruck look soon overtook his face.

"Where did you get that?" Galopin shouted.

"It was in Pryce's room" Cesar said quickly, overlooking the detail that he had taken it from Pryce's body. "This is photo of you isn't it? Why does Pryce have a photo of you?

Galopin stared at him icily. There was no obvious diplomatic way out of this, and Galopin seemed to know this.

"If you give me that to me. I will tell you all that I can."

Cesar believed him when he said this and gave him the photograph.

"Kenneth Pryce was my friend, we fought the fascists together in Spain. He was a foreign volunteer, and I was entrenched with the Republicans on behalf of French intelligence. This photograph was taken during that time."

"Who is the other man in the photograph? Someone else I should know about?"

"No," Galopin said with a shake of his head.

"What is *this*? What are you doing here Major?"

Galopin sighed, the exterior he had spent the night maintaining was falling, and it was gradually becoming easier to get him to reveal his secrets "Decarli invited me, and that is the truth."

"Why?"

"He had a job for me to do, that is all I will say on the matter."

"What job?"

"I said that is all I'll say on the matter" Galopin repeated forcefully.

Cesar knew that he could neither persuade nor intimidate Galopin into telling him details that he was truly unwilling to give. He was the type of individual who would've died first, so Cesar just moved on. "How did you know Decarli?"

"I met him in early 1937, when Franco was trying to capture Madrid again, and this time he had Mussolini's soldiers and colonial troops from Morocco. The Republicans needed proper arms, but the prospects for armaments were limited to what could be scavenged, the shipments that the Mexican and Soviet governments were able to get through, and the black market."

"When it came to the black market, there were a number of arms dealers in Europe who it was believed would be able to exceed expectations. Alexander Decarli was on that list. I along with four other men were sent to Switzerland to meet with Decarli. Pryce was one of the four men."

"Who were the others?"

"Two belonged to the Spanish Republican Armed Forces, officers, they were running the show. Another was a Czech Marxist who was familiar with smuggling. They all were killed during the war, Pryce and I are the only survivors of-"

Galopin stopped himself midsentence as he realized what he was about to say, he closed his mouth and looked over Cesar's shoulder with a bothered look. He gritted his teeth for a few moments before looking back at Cesar with a steadied expression. "Pryce and I were the only survivors of the delegation" he said, mildly.

"Decarli supplied weapons to the Republican cause?"

"To a limited degree. He was quite generous and pragmatic, even though I suspected he didn't actually care for the cause. In any case, Decarli believed that I was reliable, and suggested that I could potentially be of use to him in future endeavors. I refused, telling him that I was a soldier, not a mercenary or some gangster. But when he contacted me a few months ago and explained his preposition, I knew that I could not refuse it."

"That still doesn't explain Pryce? Why was he invited?"

"Decarli invited him as part of the arrangement that was made. He was to be my second. If I died, Pryce would take my place."

Cesar remembered Melikov, and how he claimed to have been hired for a similar function.

"And you have no desire to tell me what this job is?"

"No, I do not."

"Even if it could mean achieving justice for Pryce?"

Galopin gave him a look that Cesar hoped he would never see again "I think it is time you and I depart from each other."

"Understood" Cesar said hastily. He turned and made way for the door to the corridor.

"Mondragon!"

Cesar stopped walking as Galopin shouted his name.

"When I find out who killed Kenneth, I will be doing the same to him. And if you in anyway try to prevent that, I will take action that will make it so you are unable to prevent me."

Cesar said nothing.

"Leave me!"

He left the room as fast as he could. Once he had put distance between himself and Galopin, he allowed himself a minute for contemplation and to catch his breath. He found contemplation difficult as the night's events were quickly becoming onerous for him, so he returned to his search for the staffroom. Now with better light, he accessed the map and found a quick route to his destination.

When Cesar entered the Hotel Geraldine's staff room, he found a familiar man in a butler's uniform. The man stood patiently with his arms behind his back and looked to be waiting for somebody.

"Who are you?" Cesar blurted out.

He looked at Cesar in surprise. "Err…My name is Christoph, I served you dinner."

"Oh…Yes, I remember…Where is-"

Another door connected to the staff room opened, Valencia and Doctor Gounelle came out from it.

"Ah! There you are Cesar. Good." Valencia said brightly. "Doctor Gounelle and I were able to identify the poison that was used to kill my father."

Cesar thought of the secret room he had found and the secret he had learned about Galopin and Pryce. He would wait till he and Valencia were alone before confronting her "Please tell me."

"I will let Doctor Gounelle explain."

The Doctor softly cleared his throat before he began. "It is an obscure poison, you see. One that does not even have a proper name. Thankfully I have a colleague from Belgium who specializes in rare poisons and diseases, and I have a copy of his book."

"How do you know what type of poison it is if it doesn't have a name?" Cesar asked.

"It lacks a proper name, but that does not mean there are no names for it. The Dutch commonly call it *'Langzaam Dood Toxine'* or 'Slow Death Toxin.' It's harvested from a rare plant found in the Dutch East Indies, New Guinea to be precise. It is exceedingly difficult to find the toxin in Europe, there are even some who claim it doesn't exist. It is indeed real though, and what little of it there is was brought here by Dutch ships."

"Why is it called 'the Slow Death Toxin?'"

"Not for the reason you may think, the toxin has a delayed effect and it takes forty to fifty minutes to kill a fully grown adult. However, there are those who take the name of the toxin to mean that it produces a slow and painful death. But this is not the case, once the toxin takes effect, whoever has taken it will be dead within a minute's time."

"It is still painful though?"

Gounelle cast a glance towards Valencia before he responded "It is poison and therefore unpleasant by its very composition. But this particular poison is not meant to maximize or prolong pain."

"I take comfort in knowing my father did not suffer more than necessary" Valencia said soberly. "What's more, we now know he consumed the poison forty or fifty minutes before he died. Surely that must be useful Cesar?

"Yes, I…think it is."

"Christoph, what are you doing here?" Valencia said, having just noticed him.

"Miss Decarli, I sincerely beg your pardon, but I felt obligated to inform you that several of the domestic staff have gone."

"They've gone? Gone where?"

"Away from here. They had been unsettled to learn Mister Decarli had died and that the cause of death was possibly poison. When one of them reported the sound of gunshots coming from the library, they became inconsolably frightened. I took matters into my own hands and dismissed several of them."

"I see, and what staff remain?"

"Aside from myself? I believe Brigitte and Anna are still here, as are the kitchen staff, they've finished cleaning the kitchen and are now gambling. Nicolas is still at the front desk of course, indifferent to everything that occurs around him. And I suspect the groundskeeper Giovanni is here somewhere."

"Thank you for bringing this to my attention, and I believe you acted appropriately. Fortunately, this amounts to a small inconvenience. Please tell all who remain that they have performed splendidly tonight and that they will be rewarded afterwards."

"And what of those that've been dismissed?"

"They as well will receive the appropriate compensation. Let there be no ill-will towards them."

"Very good Miss Decarli. Now if I may, I believe I should return to my rituals."

"You may."

Christoph left.

"Cesar, I neglected to ask how you're meeting with Mister Pryce went?"

"Pryce is dead."

Valencia's face fell. Doctor Gounelle's perpetually grim expression simply became grimmer.

"Pryce is dead. My God…How?"

"I found him in his room, he'd been stabbed."

"This night just keeps getting worse it would seem" Valencia said heavily. "Doctor Gounelle, you have been excellent thus far. But it is my regret that I must ask you to examine another body."

"If I must, I shall." The doctor left.

"Why have Pryce examined?" Cesar asked Valencia. "His cause of death is evident, he's been stabbed."

"Is it not possible that he was stabbed afterwards to conceal the actual method by which he was killed?"

He doubted that, but he was also in no position to declare it impossible "I've never heard of such a thing, but I suppose that's… plausible."

She smirked at this. "Mister Mondragon, I'd expect a man in your profession to be less deceivable."

He was taken aback by this statement and said nothing initially "Explain what you mean."

"What reason do I have to believe Pryce was killed by anything other than a stabbing? If you indeed found him in that state?"

He stared at her "None, that I know of."

"I requested that Doctor Gounelle examine Pryce's body so that he may leave the room."

"And why would you need him to leave the room?"

"So that you may inform me of what you found in Pryce's room. And do not bother asking me how I know that you found something worthwhile, you simply have that look about you."

She looked at him expectantly, and he knew he had to say something. "I found a photo of Galopin on Pryce's person."

"You found what?" Valencia said, putting on the appearance of someone who did not expect such information. "Why would Pryce have a photo of Galopin?"

"It was a photo of Galopin during his time with the Republicans in Spain. Pryce was of course a photographer, and it so happens that he too volunteered for the Republicans in Spain. They fought alongside each other."

"You did not discern all of that from a photograph" Valencia said with sharp suspicion.

"Galopin told me what I was unable to piece together. He also told me that he and Pryce were hired by your father, he brought them to the Geraldine to complete a job for him."

"Galopin told you this?" Valencia said, a flicker of disbelief in her voice.

"He…Yes" Cesar said slowly.

"And you don't believe he was lying to you?" she said, suddenly speaking at an unusually fast pace.

"I'm very good at knowing when someone is lying and when they're telling the truth. Galopin was telling the truth."

"And what was this job that my father intended for the two of them?"

"I could not convince Galopin to tell me."

Valencia growled "This is aggravating. All night we have been trying to ascertain answers, but we only end up with more questions."

Cesar did not answer and instead just stared at her.

"Why are you looking at me like that?" she said sternly.

"You impress me" Cesar said dryly.

She smiled charmingly and raised an eyebrow at him, perhaps thinking she was being complimented. "I impress you?"

"Yes," Cesar said boldly. "I've met many people who've made an act of knowing less than they actually do, but none have been so convincing as you."

Her charming smile vanished quickly. He gave her a hard look.

"Mister Mondragon, do you have something you would like to say to me?" she asked icily.

"It's time for you tell me all that you really know."

"You will need to be more specific as I do not know what you are referring to."

Cesar said nothing as he pulled out the map of the hotel that he took from the secret room downstairs. He held both ends of it and showed it to her. Valencia looked at the map mildly "A map of the Geraldine. Fascinating, where did you find that?"

He sighed sadly, understanding that she wouldn't break easily. He would have to do something that he took no pleasure in.

Handing the map to Valencia, he reached into his sleeve and carefully took out the note Alexander had written for his daughter. He held the letter in one hand as he showed it to Valencia.

She looked at the letter mortified and then looked at Cesar with fury in her eyes, this was the first time tonight he had seen her so angry.

"Give that to me!" she said fiercely, snatching the letter from his hand.

They both stared at each other, each of them aware that she had let down her defenses.

"You know where I found this letter, you know what I've seen. And now it is time for you to tell me what you know."

"You seem to have an idea of what it is that I know" she said scathingly. "Suppose that you tell me that idea, and if it is correct, I will tell you."

"Very well, I have reason to believe that your father carefully planned for the night's events, possibly even intending for himself to be killed in the process. I know that you know just as much as he did before his death. I know that in your letters to each other, you both refer to an unidentified 'he' that seems to feature prominently in your father's plans. And I think you know which of the seven individuals that were brought here tonight, whether they be presently living or presently dead, is responsible for poisoning your father."

She said nothing.

"I also suspect that you know why he killed your father."

She still said nothing.

"Miss Decarli, do you know who killed your father?"

She gave him a look that was partially impressed "Yes I do, and I think you do as well."

"Why did he…"

They were interrupted by the door to the staffroom swinging open. Cesar acted reflexively, drawing his LeMat revolver and pointing it at the person who stood in the doorway.

"No! Don't shoot me!" Rombauer said frantically.

"Doctor Rombauer" Valencia said, concern in her voice.

"Herr Mondragon, Fraulein Decarli! I am so thankful to have found you, I was looking for you and heard your voices in this room!" His voice was fearful and desperate, but also filled with elation to see Cesar and Valencia.

"You must please help, we have to hurry! It's Biassiano!"

"What has Biassiano done?" Cesar said quickly.

"He has attacked Mister Dickerson."

"Biassiano attacked Dickerson?" Cesar asked, his mind going to the dossier on Dickerson he had found in Biassiano's room.

"Yes, he struck him with a fire poker! And I ran to find somebody!"

"Why did Biassiano attack Dickerson?"

"I do not know! Biassiano said that Dickerson stole something from him."

Cesar thought for a moment, aware of the dossier in his possession. Was this his fault?

"Mondragon, you must help! If something is not done, Biassiano will kill Dickerson!"

"Doctor Rombauer, remain calm. Tell me where they are."

"They are in the drawing room, that is where the attack happened."

"Let's get to the drawing room then."

"No, I do not wish to go back" Rombauer said, still very afraid.

"You will be safe with me, now come along."

"I do not want to go back to the drawing room!"

Just when Cesar felt like shouting at Rombauer, Valencia intervened.

"I will take Doctor Rombauer to his room, Cesar. Please go and help Mister Dickerson."

Cesar and Valencia took a moment to look at each other, in that moment they managed to convey that neither of them was finished with the other. Not wasting any more time, Cesar took off and hurried in the direction of the drawing room.

Chapter 9
A Dwindling Party

Cesar cautiously entered the drawing room. There was no sight of either Biassiano or Dickerson when he arrived there. He looked in the side room where Decarli had died, but all that was there was Decarli's body with a tarp over it. He went back into the drawing room where he heard a gunshot somewhere in the distance.

"Oh great," he muttered.

He went back out into the halls and went towards where he believed the gunshot had come from. He soon came across four men dressed in white kitchen uniforms running in the opposite direction of him, obviously the kitchen staff. Cesar grabbed one of them and held him against the wall.

"Let me go!"

"What are you running from?

"They're in the wine cellar!"

"Who?"

"The man from Italy and two others! The Italian shot at us when we went to the cellar!"

"Who're the two with him?"

"The American and another who I don't know!"

Cesar released him and said "Go." The cook ran off.

Cesar arrived in the kitchen, the sounds of shouting led him to a darkly lit doorway. He drew his revolver and entered the doorway, descending a set of stone stairs.

"Biassiano!" he shouted down into the darkness.

"Who's there!?" said the familiar voice of the fascist.

"It's Mondragon! I'm coming down there!"

A shot from a gun struck the bottom of the stairs "Go away you ingrate!"

Cesar quickly descended the rest of the stairs down into the wine cellar, his revolver pointed in front of him. Francis Edmund Dickerson was tied to a chair, his glasses had been cracked and his face was bruised. Biassiano took cover behind him, in his hand was a Beretta pistol that he had pointed towards Dickerson's head. On the floor near them was Von Strichtenheimer, his hands had been bound and his bloody face showed that he had been beaten far worse than Dickerson.

"You're willing to die to save the life of this cretinous yank!?" Biassiano snarled. "You are a fool!"

"I just want to know why you're doing this" Cesar said coolly.

"This American has been an impediment to my objective, therefore I am interrogating him so that I may understand his motivations."

"What about him?" Cesar pointed to Von Strichtenheimer.

"That *imbecille* came down here on his own, interrupted my interrogation to try and attack me. I do not know why."

Cesar didn't waste time trying to make sense of any of this "You mentioned an objective? What objective?"

"Rombauer" Dickerson said.

"Quiet!" Biassiano hissed, placing the Berretta against Dickerson's face. The American seethed as he felt the hot barrel of the recently fired gun.

"What do you want with Rombauer?"

"Enough!" Biassiano snapped, pulling Dickerson's head back and pointing the gun at the top of his head "Put your gun on the ground or I will kill Dickerson!"

"As you insist" Cesar said smoothly, carefully placing his revolver on the ground.

Biassiano grinned victoriously and emerged from behind Dickerson, raising his gun towards Cesar. At the same time, Cesar retrieved the M1911 pistol that was tucked into the back of his pants, drew on Biassiano faster, and fired once. Biassiano shouted and fell to the ground as he was shot in the chest.

"No!" Biassiano screamed wrathfully, refusing to accept his defeat. He made a strenuous effort to aim his Beretta at Cesar.

However, Cesar had already picked his revolver up from off the floor, aimed it towards Biassiano, and fired again. The bullet scrapped the bottom of Biassiano's hand and entered the bottom of his arm. He involuntarily yelled out in pain and grabbed his arm, the Beretta falling from his hand.

Cesar approached the fallen fascist with his revolver still equipped, he kicked the Beretta away.

"Anything else you'd like to try?" Cesar asked.

Biassiano's uninjured left fist instinctively went into a pocket on his coat, Cesar thought that was curious.

"Is there something in your pocket?"

"Go to hell!"

Cesar pointed his revolver in the direction of Biassiano's head "I could kill you and look myself."

Biassiano growled in anger and removed his clenched fist from his pocket. Cesar placed his foot on the Italian's left arm, he unclenched his hand. There was a crumpled-up piece of paper in it.

"What's this?" Cesar said, picking the paper up and uncrumpling it.

Pietro Biassiano,

I am writing to inform you that the commission once again has need of you. I have consulted with my German counterpart and he concurs that you are suited to the task we have in mind.

There is a Doctor Ludwig Rombauer who resides in Sweden. The Germans assert that he was an important contributor to their development and production of armaments in the Great War, and that he would be useful again.

But the Doctor Rombauer is not a proud member of the German nation, nor does he have a favorable opinion of the government in Berlin. From this we can assume he has the equivalent lack of respect for Il Duce and our cause.

This is not to say that his loyalty is to the democracies in the west or the communist barbarians. He is a capitalist whose chief concerns are his own mercenary interests. To that end, he has resigned himself to his present status as a beneficiary of the government in Sweden, who're neutral and have put his knowledge towards non-military applications (That we know of.)

Your base objective is to ensure that he will never be of use to our enemies in Britain and France, as they are in more need of him more than we are. If we are fated to conduct the coming war without the aid of Ludwig Rombauer, then we will do so gallantly. It remains though, that the optimum outcome would be a war with Ludwig Rombauer on the side of the Italian Empire and the Third Reich.

That is why your ideal objective would be to bring him over to our effort. He must be persuaded that his best mercenary interests lie with Italy and Germany, with the Pact of Steel that in the next ten years will do away with the old European order and establish a newer, greater one.

Make him aware of the certainty of this victory and present him with the opportunity to be one of the people who benefits from it.

If he cannot be brought over to the correct thinking, then measures to take him to Italy by force are an option, but it will be your responsibility to decide whether that's possible or even necessary, and this commission trusts in your judgment.

If you cannot fulfill your ideal objective, then your base objective remains your prime objective. Ludwig Rombauer must not fall into possession of the Anglo-French alliance or any other power that is hostile to the ambitions and pursuits of our ascendant order. This means elimination of him.

Once this is done, you will be able to return to your district in Sicily and resume your perfect duties.

All further information is to be made available through your proper contacts.

ADDENDUM: Keep this document separate from any other documents you possess. I shall remind you what happened last year when one of our assets carried all his documents in a satchel.

Cordiali Saluti
Colonnello Comandante Vittore Alfano

Cesar hurriedly read the letter twice, not fully sure of what he was reading. He placed it into his pocket, it would be addressed in time.

Cesar noticed a knife on the floor, not the pristine dagger Biassiano had earlier used to intimidate Von Strichtenheimer, but a common hunting knife. Cesar picked up the knife and used it to cut Von Strichtenheimer's bounds. He then moved to Dickerson to cut his bounds as well.

"What an awful night this has been" Dickerson said tiredly as he stood up from the chair.

"It's almost over Mister Dickerson" Cesar said as he tossed the knife on the ground "I'll soon be able to piece together what's happened."

"Where's Doctor Rombauer?"

"He's with Miss Decarli, they — *What are you doing!?*"

Cesar couldn't stop himself from shouting. Von Strichtenheimer was kneeling over Biassiano, he had the hunting knife raised in the air. He lunged towards Von Strichtenheimer but was not able to stop him from plunging the knife into Biassiano's neck. Rather than pull the knife out for a second strike, Von Strichtenheimer kept the knife in Biassiano's neck and twisted the blade around. Cesar attempted to no avail to wrestle him into submission.

Dickerson soon ran over and assisted Cesar in restraining Von Strichtenheimer. Even with two of them working to overpower him, it proved to be a difficult task. To Cesar, it felt like there was some strange force that drove Von Strichtenheimer to kill Biassiano, and that he and Dickerson were struggling against that force.

Cesar eventually had the sense to kick Von Strichtenheimer in the shin. Dickerson was then able to pry the hunting knife from his hands and throw it away. Cesar tossed the disarmed man across the stone floor.

Cesar realized too late that he had tossed Von Strichtenheimer near where Biassiano's Beretta lay on the floor. The man picked up the Beretta and fired one shot towards Cesar's legs.

The bullet missed Cesar's left knee, he hurled himself across the room to escape Von Strichtenheimer's line of fire.

Now on his feet, Von Strichtenheimer fired another shot in Dickerson's direction. The bullet broke a wine bottle behind the American, making him to drop to the ground.

Von Strichtenheimer ran toward the cellar stars, firing the Beretta erratically at the walls to prevent Cesar and Dickerson from pursuing him. As he scrambled up to the stairs, he took one look behind him and roared "Stay away from me!" His voice was inhuman, as if something had been unleashed inside him. He climbed the rest of the cellar stairs and vanished from sight.

Cesar looked to where Pietro Biassiano lay on the ground, the once mighty and self-satisfied fascist looked up at the ceiling with a glazed look in his eyes. His face, clothes, and the ground beneath him were stained with the blood from his catastrophic neck wound. Von Strichtenheimer had cut both the blood arteries in the neck, which ensured that Biassiano's death came quickly. Now four had been killed at the Hotel Geraldine.

"What the hell is going on here!?" Dickerson shouted.

Cesar pointed his revolver at the American "Don't move."

"What-" Dickerson sputtered. "What are you-"

"I'm through with the game that is being played here tonight. Tell me what you're doing here, tell me about Biassiano and Rombauer. You have ten seconds to do so or else I'll shoot you in the foot."

Dickerson received the message clearly and nodded to show his cooperation "Yes, yes, I shall. Just…let me reach into my pocket."

He reached into his vest and pulled out a set of documents that looked like a booklet of identification papers. He opened the booklet and showed its contents to Cesar. "I work for the United States Department of State."

Cesar peered at the booklet "Why? What are you doing here?"

"I'm here for Doctor Ludwig Rombauer and to ensure that his expertise as a military engineer does not fall into the hands of the governments in Germany and Italy."

"Biassiano was here for the opposite end," Cesar said, hastily recalling what he had read in Biassiano's letter, "To bring him to their side, or to get rid of him if it couldn't be done."

"Yes, I was sent to be a counterweight to him. That document you found on him? I had purloined it from his room and intended to show Doctor Rombauer that he was in danger. Biassiano knew what I had done and assaulted me with a fire poker."

That meant this wasn't Cesar's fault, Dickerson had also been to Biassiano's room at some point during the night and had also taken something from him.

"How much did Decarli know about this?"

"Alexander? My understanding is that he knew about the full of it. He contacted numerous people in France and Britain, as well as my own country. He told them that Rombauer would be attending a function at a designated time and place, that Biassiano would also be attending with Rombauer in mind and asked if they'd like a representative of the west to attend."

Cesar was speechless. He put his revolver back in his coat and went towards the cellar door. "Come with me."

"Come with you where?" Dickerson asked.

"Valencia is with Doctor Rombauer in his room. She's going to explain herself to me."

Dickerson followed Cesar out of the wine cellar and down the hotel's corridors as he retraced his steps back to Rombauer's room. The American was oddly quiet, and a few times Cesar looked around to make sure he was still there walking behind him.

Cesar eventually had a question "Why'd the State Department send you? And not someone…"

"Younger?" Dickerson asked pleasantly. "I take no offense, I'm not a spring chicken by any stretch of the imagination. I am, however, a victim of my own success. I've been doing this for some time, and I've worked my fair share of miracles. When this assignment came up, I seemed the perfect candidate. "

"Biassiano's dead, so I suppose your work here is done," Cesar suggested.

"I shall be staying here for the duration of the night, or morning, more precisely. I have an inkling all is not yet well, and I don't just mean the unsolved murders."

It took Cesar a few moments to register what Dickerson had just said "Then what do you mean?" he asked lightly.

"The hotel has a public telephone room near the lobby. I earlier overheard Biassiano making a call, he was talking quietly in his native Italian, so I couldn't make out…But I didn't like the sound of it."

Cesar had no further questions. Biassiano making a phone call didn't strike him as something that warranted being too concerned about.

When they arrived at Rombauer's room, Cesar noticed how quiet it was. Were

Rombauer and Valencia sitting in silence? He knocked on the door.

"Who's there?" said a recognizable German accent.

"It's Mondragon. Let me in, Ludwig."

He was greeted by the sound of someone scurrying up to and hastily unlocking the door. It opened to reveal an immensely relieved looking Rombauer.

"Oh *Herr* Mondragon. Please come in, and *Herr* Dickerson! I'm pleased you're alright, sir."

"I return your sentiments, Doctor," Dickerson said.

Valencia was nowhere to be seen, much to Cesar's annoyance.

"Where is she?" he asked Rombauer.

"*Fraulein* Decarli? I do not know."

"What do you mean you don't know?" Cesar said sharply. "She just walked off without saying anything?"

Rombauer lowered his head slightly, as if he was embarrassed "After we arrived, she suggested that I go to the restroom and splash water on my face. When I came back, I found that she left without a sound."

"She said that he would stay here with you," Cesar said, unintentionally directing his indignation to Rombauer.

The German engineer looked at a loss for words. "I…I'm sorry, but I can't answer for what she does."

"I'm not sure if you've caught on by now Mondragon," Dickerson said, "But she has not been terribly truthful with you."

Cesar looked back and forth a few times between Dickerson and Rombauer. It didn't take long for his next order of course of action to become apparent.

"I need to find Galopin or Von Strichtenheimer," he announced.

"Galopin or Von Strichtenheimer?" Dickerson asked.

"Or both of them."

"Whatever for?"

"Because unless I'm somehow mistaken, one of them killed Alexander Decarli."

Dickerson and Rombauer exchanged a surprised look.

"Uh…Doctor Rombauer and I shall remain here then, yes?"

Cesar gave a quick nod of the head "Yes, and you should barricade the door to this room."

"Quite right."

"I would also barricade that armoire."

Rombauer looked at the armoire with alarmed confusion, Dickerson understood just enough to not argue with Cesar. "Yes. We can do that."

Dickerson wished Cesar luck as he exited Rombauer's room.

Cesar took out the map and found that Galopin's room was on the ground floor near the lobby. He went downstairs and found the corridor it was in. He unlocked the door with the master key and slowly began to open it, anxiously anticipating the moment the French soldier would break the door down on top of him… but of course Galopin wasn't in there.

He searched the room but found nothing in there that would've belonged to Galopin as opposed to the hotel. Had Galopin arrived with no belongings? He perhaps possessed the soldier's sensibility to travel light, carry only a few necessities. If he needed anything else, he'd procure it while in the field.

How many times during the Great War had Galopin ventured into No-man's-land under the cover of darkness, taking with him only a knife and a tin of beef?

Cesar's thoughts were interrupted by the sound he least wanted in the world to hear, which was the sound of the door to the room opening. He spun around, expecting to see Galopin.

Instead, it was Felix von Strichtenheimer who stood in the doorway. The Austrian aristocrat stared stunned at Cesar for only a moment. "This isn't your room."

"Nor is it yours," Cesar responded swiftly.

"This is the French officer's room, should I tell him you've been here?"

"I suggest we go together and tell him we both let ourselves in," Cesar proposed tactfully.

Von Strichtenheimer was quiet "An impasse then…Shall I close the door?"

"Please."

It was better if Galopin caught them both, they would concoct a story. They heard strange noises and found the door to his room unlocked. It would sound more plausible coming from two people rather than one.

Von Strichtenheimer stood facing the closed door. The awkwardness of the situation made him unsure of how to begin. Cesar began for him.

"You killed Biassiano."

This prompted Von Strichtenheimer to turn around "He deserved to die," he exclaimed, more viscerally than he perhaps intended.

Cesar didn't disagree. "You stabbed in the neck while he was on the ground. Not exactly sporting, is it?"

The Austrian aristocrat closed his eyes and made an expression, one that could've almost been shame. "He had brutalized me, and Dickerson, and was prepared to kill you. He had gone too far… and subsequently so did I."

Cesar opted to be open with this man, in the hope that it would incline him to reveal his own secrets. "I'm no more a saint than you are, I've also killed under extremely questionable conditions."

"If you were the authorities, you'd still be obligated to arrest me," Von Strichtenheimer pointed out.

"Thankfully, I'm not the authorities."

They exchanged a look of understanding.

"Why were you down there with him and Dickerson?

"I was coming to Mr. Dickerson's aid, the same as you."

A convenient explanation. "I witnessed the altercation you and Biassiano had earlier, on the third floor."

Von Strichtenheimer looked unnerved and made little effort to hide it. "You saw that?"

"I'm afraid I'm good at remaining unseen. You both mentioned that you were here for one man. In the case of Biassiano, I now know that one man to be Doctor Rombauer. In your case, I'm less than certain and compelled to ask."

Von Strichtenheimer gave Cesar an acerbic look, one that turned to hesitation, and then to resignation.

"I've been investigating Decarli."

Cesar was greatly uncertain this was the case. "And why's that?"

"I'm rather like you, I possess the predisposition to learn the truth of things. Sometimes I do it for money, but I'll also do it of my own volition."

If he was telling the truth, then Cesar may as well learn more. "Would you like to share with me what you know?"

"I think I know who killed him."

"Who?" Cesar said quickly.

"Galopin."

Cesar had deemed Von Strichtenheimer and Galopin the most likely to have killed Alexander Decarli, and now one of them was claiming the other was responsible.

"How do you know that?"

"I think I should explain everything," Von Strichtenheimer said earnestly.

"Then do so."

Von Strichtenheimer looked cautiously at the door behind him, troubled by the thought of anyone else eavesdropping. He turned his attention back to Cesar and took care not to speak louder than was necessary.

"Decarli and his daughter arranged this event, and invited all eight of us here, with one purpose in mind, and that was to be rid of those who were a liability to him."

Under normal circumstances, the accusation that your night's host had brought his guests here to orchestrate multiple murders would've been incredibly jarring. In the past several hours, that host and three others had died, and a web of secrecy and subterfuge had revealed itself. Therefore, the circumstances were less than normal.

Cesar did, however, possess the intuitive feeling that Von Strichtenheimer's accusation was unlikely. "He brought us here to kill us?"

"Not all of us, Dickerson and Rombauer I believed he intended to spare. He only wanted them here so he could ensure Biassiano's attendance."

"Was Biassiano his main target?"

Von Strichtenheimer looked uncertain "Ehm…Possibly, yes. He was one of the men Decarli most intended to kill, although I don't know that Decarli prioritized him over the others."

"What others? Who else was he planning to kill?"

"The only other four I'm sure of are Galopin and Pryce, as well as you and me."

The news that Decarli wanted to kill him was bewildering to Cesar. The possibility of it crossed his mind at one point, but that was unimportant. For nearly all his adult life, he had approached every situation with the understanding that anyone he met had the potential to plot his death.

It was always in the back of his head, along with the possibility that it might rain while he was traveling. But apart from that general caution he exercised, Cesar never thought it extremely likely that Decarli had invited him here to die.

It was wrong somehow…too vulgar, too simple.

"I see you're skeptical," Von Strichtenheimer said, reading Cesar's face.

"Why does he want to kill me?"

"You're a detective right, you heard Decarli's name before?"

Cesar thought back to where it all began in 1937, the mysterious case of Antonin Rocca. The Marseille gangster who declared to Cesar that Alexander Decarli had hired him to commit a murder, and then abandoned him to take the fall for it.

"And how would you know that?" Cesar was more curious than suspicious as to how Von Strichtenheimer knew this.

"Two years ago? When you went to Venice and asked those men about Antonin Rocca?"

Cesar was so unprepared for what Von Strichtenheimer just said that he involuntarily took a step back. He assumed a defensive stance and resisted the impulse to go for his gun but kept his right hand ready to draw if need be.

It was uncharacteristic of him to show his hand in such a way, but Von Strichtenheimer knowing something he shouldn't have had rattled him.

Von Strichtenheimer had remained passive and only barely reacted to Cesar's display of agitation "What are you doing?" he asked in a cool and steady voice.

"How do you know that!?" Cesar sneered.

"As I said, I'm an investigator like you, and during my investigation of Decarli I also found myself looking into what occurred with Rocca. I spoke to many of the same people as you did, and your name was used. I think I even saw you in Venice at one point."

This straightforward explanation soothed Cesar, he relaxed his posture but remained on guard.

Von Strichtenheimer gestured towards Cesar "That's what you and I have in common. We're both men who took an interest in Decarli. He didn't appreciate it and was concerned we would look too deep."

"What about Biassiano, Galopin and Pryce?"

"Biassiano knew of Decarli's support for the Republican cause in Spain through a source in Switzerland and was extorting him using the Camorra as an intermediary."

"He was extorting Decarli over his Spanish Civil War affiliations?" Cesar asked. Of all the secrets he had uncovered tonight, he'd seen none that indicated as much.

"Yes, now that the Nationalists control Spain, he wanted to keep those affiliations as little known as possible. Likely to avoid any potential complications to his affairs in that country. It wasn't necessary for him to erase every trace, only enough to leave room for deniability."

"Galopin and Pryce fought for the Republican Cause in Spain," Cesar volunteered, wondering again if Spain was major component in this mystery.

"I'm aware," Von Strichtenheimer said with a nod. "Pryce as a foreign volunteer, Galopin as part of a team of 'observers' sent by the French. And they both met Decarli at some point during the war, I believe it was for an arms deal or some such business."

Von Strichtenheimer knowing all this gave credence to his assertions, but Cesar was still suspicious of what he was hearing.

"Their ability to name him as a Republican supporter earned them places on his list of liabilities." Von Strichtenheimer continued. "He lured Galopin and Pryce here to have them do his dirty work, but he planned to get rid of them as well. You, I, and Biassiano were intended to die at their hands. Rombauer was brought here to ensure Biassiano's attendance, and Rombauer's attendance meant Dickerson had to be in attendance as well."

Von Strichtenheimer crossed his arms as if he were a lawyer delivering his closing arguments "Galopin found out and derailed Decarli's plans by poisoning him."

"That just leaves Melikov."

The expression Von Strichtenheimer made indicated he had

temporarily forgotten the dead Russian. "Ah of course…he puzzles me the most."

"I suspect Pryce of killing him."

"What makes you suspect that?"

"I was there when Melikov was murdered. His killer broke a window from the outside and tossed in a grenade. It couldn't've been Galopin because I encountered him outside the library door minutes afterwards. I then observed that Pryce was in possession of the pin to a grenade."

"That would fit, my best theory is that Melikov was supposed to kill Galopin and Pryce. After Galopin poisoned Decarli, Pryce went to dispose of Melikov."

"Melikov also confessed to me that he was an assassin."

Von Strichtenheimer gave a pleased grin "My theory is vindicated then."

"Except Melikov didn't tell me he was hired by Decarli."

Von Strichtenheimer's grin receded "Oh no?"

"He told me he was hired killer, yes. But instead claimed he was hired by one of the others here tonight. He said that this person was the one who killed Decarli, and that he was only there to assist them or kill Decarli should they fail."

Von Strichtenheimer listened to this with quiet patience, never daring to interrupt. Once it was clear Cesar was finished, he then asked, "And you believed him?"

Cesar took this question to heart. Melikov was such a stoic and strange individual, that there was little in the way of behavioral tells to determine whether he was genuine. He could've claimed responsibility for the Reichstag fire and he would've done so with the same inscrutable seriousness.

But yes, Cesar did believe him at the time.

"He had the poison that was likely used to kill Decarli."

"I see."

Von Strichtenheimer's body language gave little hint that he was distressed by his hypothesis being contradicted. "Forgive me, but might I ask…Did he tell anyone else this?"

"Only Miss Decarli."

"When did he tell her?"

"He told us togeth – " He stopped midsentence. "…Together."

It was only as Cesar finished this sentence that he realized the significance of it. Valencia had been in the room when Melikov delivered his story, which cast it in doubt. If Melikov had been working for the Decarlis, then he wouldn't tell Cesar as much in front of Valencia Decarli.

Von Strichtenheimer gave him a knowing look. He could tell that Cesar was taking seriously all that had just been said.

"Decarli went to all these lengths…" Cesar said slowly, "…And planned the deaths of five men, because he was determined to eliminate anyone that could potentially link him to the war in Spain?"

"Europe is changing, you do realize that? Italy, Germany, Hungary, Portugal, and now Spain. The old way of doing things is being swept away by men in colored shirts."

"The future is fascist?" Cesar suggested. He met those who shared the opinion.

"Perhaps Decarli thought as much, and perhaps he…"

Von Strichtenheimer stopped abruptly…Because he heard the same thing that Cesar did.

They were both hearing voices in the distance, male voices Cesar couldn't recognize, and it sounded like they were arguing.

And then they heard a gunshot.

Chapter 10
Uninvited Guests

Cesar's estimation was that the gunshot they heard came from the lobby, or at least the direction of the lobby. Von Strichtenheimer was happy to let him lead the way. Cesar took out his revolver as they made their way down the corridor. It wasn't only the threat of what awaited in the lobby that made Cesar want to be armed, but the possible threat of Von Strichtenheimer who followed behind him.

In the lobby they found Christoph standing in place, looking as if he was afraid to move.

"Christoph," Cesar called out.

The butler made a noise of fright and spun around to see who was walking towards him, he looked relieved to see it was Cesar "Oh, it's just you, sir."

"Has someone been shot?"

Christoph gaped at him, looking fearful again "I…I don't know. Has someone?"

Cesar quietly stared at him for a few moments, he could somehow feel the exasperation and incredulity oozing out of the pores of his face "You didn't hear the gunshot a minute ago?" he asked as mildly as he could manage.

A look of sudden awareness spread across Christoph's face "Oh! No one was shot sir, they fired a shot into the ceiling-"

"Who did!?" Cesar shouted, at his wit's end.

Christoph blinked multiple times, being shouted at seemed to have slid his mind firmly back into place. "A group of men, they barged in and demanded information about the event being held here. The concierge summoned me, and I tried to convince them to leave, but this made them hostile. One of them fired a gun in the air and threatened to shoot me."

Cesar looked back at Von Strichtenheimer, and the two men read each other's looks. The inexplicable arrival of an armed group of men wasn't a development either of them was expecting.

He looked back towards Christoph "What men? Who are they?"

"I didn't think to ask them sir, they didn't give me the opportunity as they made threats against the concierge and I."

"What concierge?" Von Strichtenheimer asked.

They all looked at the front desk to see that no one was there.

"Nicolas, where are you!?" Christoph snapped.

The concierge, Nicolas, jumped up from his place behind the front desk. It was the same one that Cesar had first encountered when he arrived, however many hours ago that was. Nicolas looked unsettled, but not quite as petrified as Christoph. He scanned the lobby for any signs of further hostility. It took him only a few moments to recover, he brushed his clothes off and put his hands behind his back, looking most unaffected.

A look of annoyance flashed across Christoph's face as he looked away from the front desk. "As you can see, we are both quite unharmed, sir," he remarked to Cesar.

"These men, where did they go?"

"What? Oh…I directed them towards the drawing room. No one is there, and I had to direct them somewhere to placate them."

"How many of them were there?"

"There were five."

Cesar was quiet for several moments, uncertain of what he was to do about five violent strangers. One thing of course came to mind, and it was what usually came to his mind in instances such as this. And that was to act decisively and fearlessly.

Five men? He had faced worse than that, trials and tribulations where the odds weren't in his favor. And not only did he never fail to come out in one piece, but he barely had the scars to show for it. He was either formidable, fortunate, or favored by fate.

And he wouldn't be alone this time either. He looked at Von Strichtenheimer, who knew what he was thinking and nodded at him.

Cesar made his decision. "The two of us will confront them, demand to know what they're doing here."

"What…should I do?" Christoph asked with uncertainty.

"Uh…Try to stay out of the way."

The butler sighed happily, finding a policy of avoidance to his liking.

Von Strichtenheimer was on the move. "Let's not wait any longer," he signaled for Cesar to follow. As they left, he could hear Christoph and Nicolas conversing with each other.

"What makes you so resilient!?"

"This is the position I was hired for."

As Cesar walked with Von Strichtenheimer, he thought of a way to even their odds. "We should find Galopin."

"The two of us are enough for this," the Austrian aristocrat instantly said, his tone dismissive.

"Are you sure?"

"Yes," Von Strichtenheimer said this with such certitude, that Cesar momentarily wondered if he was being overly cautious.

"Are you armed?"

Von Strichtenheimer pulled out a pistol, it looked like a Luger. Cesar felt better about their odds.

Cesar was capable in scrapes and a proficient gunfighter. He had acquired these skills as a young soldier and lawmen in Mexico and took care to maintain them in his time as a private investigator. His primary concern was whether he had enough cartridges in his coat.

It was in the corridor outside the drawing room that they

encountered what must've been one of the intruders. A strange man stood in the corridor with his hands behind his back, as if he had been ordered to stand watch.

This man had the complexion and black hair of someone of a Mediterranean extraction and wore a three-piece slate green suit. He saw Cesar and Von Strichtenheimer coming and smiled at them. A tactic to put them at ease?

"Hello gentlemen," he said cordially.f

Cesar was in no mood and pointed his LeMat Revolver at him.

The Mediterranean man responded with mild offense "What's this? You mean to shoot me?"

"I only mean to shoot you if you don't answer my questions," he said viciously, and he meant it.

"As soon as you ask one, certainly."

"What are you doing here?"

"We have business with one of the guests."

"What guest?"

The Mediterranean man tilted his head, his expression humorless. "I don't presume that it's your business," he said with distinct politeness.

Cesar's first thought was to hit the man or shoot him in his ankle. His second thought was the man's accent, which he had begun to discern. "Are you...Italian?"

The Mediterranean man looked pleased by this recognition. "Ah-ha! *Si certo!*" he placed one hand behind his back, another hand across his waste, and bowed in greeting "*Buongiorno.*"

Cesar found this man bizarre. Von Strichtenheimer aggressively advanced on him "We don't return your sentiments," he grabbed the man's suit, "You will tell us who you are, and what..."

The next few events happened in quick succession with each other. Cesar saw a figure move out of the shadows towards Von Strichtenheimer and went for his gun. Then he sensed movement from his side and turned in that direction.

He felt the pain of being struck in the face, and then felt the floor collide with him. Someone's foot was placed on his back, and his revolver was taken from his hand. Cesar knew enough to stay still. If they wanted to kill him, they would've already done so.

As he remained immobile and stared at the floor, he heard a struggle and the sound of Von Strichtenheimer's angry voice. "Don't touch me! *Abschaum!*"

He heard fists impacting with flesh and Von Strichtenheimer's pained grunting.

One of them nudged Cesar with their foot. "You may stand up now," they said. It was the Mediterranean man.

Cesar slowly got to his feet and assessed the new situation in front of him.

The Mediterranean man had taken possession of Cesar's Lemat revolver and was pointing it at him. Two new men were restraining a pacified Von Strichtenheimer.

The first one was a strong-looking, young man with dark blonde hair and an unfriendly smile on his face. The second one was older, but also smaller and thinner. He had a wispy mustache and beard and mouthful of oversized teeth, all of which made Cesar think of a rodent. Both were dressed in drab, common clothes; making them look like working-class laborers or wandering vagabonds.

The Mediterranean man gestured towards the drawing room door with the confiscated revolver. "After you."

Cesar complied and led them into the drawing room. Standing in the room was a fourth unidentified man. He was much older than the other three and had a brutal face, with beady eyes and receding light-brown hair. He wore a long gray overcoat which he had his hands in the pockets of.

"What is this? Corvo, who are these men?"

The Mediterranean man, who was apparently called Corvo, pointed at Cesar with the LeMat Revolver. "*Gli ho tolto questa pistol.*"

"Speak English," the man with the brutal face snapped.

Corvo shrugged "He already knows."

Cesar immediately began piecing things together. Corvo had spoken Italian, the brutal Italian instructed him to speak English, Corvo's response was that Cesar "already knows." Not only were these men all Italian, but they'd rather not make this abundantly clear if they could help it. This was probably to make it unclear who they were, at least for as long as they were here.

Naturally them being Italian made him think of Pietro Biassiano, who was in the wine cellar with his neck open. He thought of Biassiano's mission to "recruit" Ludwig Rombauer to the Rome-Berlin Axis.

If Cesar were to hazard a guess…These men belonged to Italian intelligence, or they were Blackshirt militia out of uniform, probably a combination of both. And they were here in conjunction with Biassiano, possibly as a support team.

The brutal Italian squinted at Cesar. "What do you have a gun for?"

"I'm a private investigator."

The brutal Italian was interested in this. "Oh yes? And are you here in that function?"

"I have no idea what I'm doing here," he confessed.

The brutal Italian stared at him. Cesar had said it in such a way that his sincerity was without doubt.

"This one had a gun too," the young blonde Italian said, holding Von Strichtenheimer's Luger.

"Another private investigator?" the brutal Italian said softly. His gaze and voice were ominous, as if he were silently threatening Cesar to tell the truth.

"You'll have to ask him," Cesar said. Von Strichtenheimer was a big boy, he could answer his own questions.

"He's got a lot of fight in him" the young blonde Italian said. "Getting him to talk will be difficult…" The look on his face was truly repulsive, "…and enjoyable."

The brutal Italian wasn't amused, "We do nothing without Capaldi's approval."

"Where is he?" Corvo asked.

"He went to Biassiano's room, it's nearby. He should be here soon."

Two minutes passed, and the door to the drawing room opened and the final member of this group of intruders revealed himself.

The man who entered must've been Capaldi, and he was unquestionably the leader of this group of intruders, Cesar was able to guess as much from the imposing way he carried himself. He was a tall, skinny, and weathered looking individual with unruly grayish-brown hair and intense, piercing eyes. His clothes were almost all black. His frock coat, vest, ties, trousers, and dress shoes being this color, the only exception the white shirt under his vest. Cesar thought of an undertaker.

This tall Italian was easily over the age of fifty, but Cesar could tell just by looking at him that he could go toe-to-toe with men half his age. He was also a Great War veteran, it was no secret. His age, the way he walked, the fierce and arduous disposition that separated him from the common masses, Cesar had seen enough American, Canadian, and European veterans of that war to recognize them on sight.

"The prefect wasn't in his room," Capaldi said as he strolled up to his men. His voice was mild-mannered, and he spoke the best English of the group.

"Who are they?" he asked, looking first at Cesar and then at Von Strichtenheimer.

"They had guns," Corvo spoke up.

"This one says he's a private investigator,'" the brutal Italian added, pointing at Cesar.

Capaldi scratched his nose, looking nonchalant. "Turina, bring him here."

The brutal Italian, named Turina, took Cesar by the arm and

lead him over to Capaldi. He was surprisingly gentle about it…
But then he kicked Cesar in the back of his leg, putting him on
his knees.

Capaldi briefly gave Turina a look of disapproval, before
turning his full attention to Cesar. "Are you a guest here?"

"Yes," Cesar said through gritted teeth, wishing to hurt Turina.

"Then perhaps you could help us find two other guests."

He pulled out two photographs and held them out in front of
Cesar. They were photographs of Pietro Biassiano and Ludwig
Rombauer.

"We know they're both attending the event here, the same as
you."

Cesar stared at the photographs for a few moments before
responding "We've seen them, but we don't know where they are."

Biassiano was dead, killed by Von Strichtenheimer. And
Rombauer was barricaded in his room. Cesar obviously wasn't
about to willingly supply this information to these men, so he
played the part of the oblivious bystander.

"You don't know where they are? I thought there was a party
being held here tonight?"

"There is - There was." Cesar stumbled over his words, "We've
since then…broken up," he finished, aware of how untrustworthy
he sounded.

"He's lying," the young blonde Italian said. "Hit him, or at least
let me."

"Be quiet Renzetti," Capaldi said firmly.

"Corvo, where are you going?" Turina said.

They all looked at Corvo, who had been heading in the direction
of the door to the side room. The same room where Alexander
Decarli's dead body lay.

"I want to see what's behind that door," Corvo answered.

Turina looked at Capaldi for instruction, Capaldi nodded at
Corvo.

Cesar thought and acted quickly, "I can tell you what's in there!" It'd be better if he told them about Decarli's body, as opposed to them discovering it for themselves.

Now they all looked at him, even Corvo who stopped walking.

"And what's that?" Capaldi said sharply, analyzing Cesar with his intense eyes.

"A dead body."

A stunned silence followed this statement. Corvo continued over to the room and went in. They waited several seconds for his return.

"Yes, he's right. There's a dead man in there, he's been covered up."

"Explain yourself," Capaldi demanded "Who is that man in there?"

"It's our host, he died," Cesar almost stopped there, but then decided to reveal the full truth "We think he's been poisoned."

Capaldi turned to the look at the side room, possibly deliberating going to inspect the body himself. "Your host?" he said as he turned back to Cesar. "Alexander Decarli is dead?"

They knew who Decarli was, or at least knew he was their host.

"The house doctor examined him, and a bottle of poison was found."

"But who killed him?"

"We can't be sure."

Capaldi's face was stern and pensive. Cesar could all but see the gears turning in his head as he was confronted with the unusual event taking place at the Geraldine.

"If Decarli invited you all here…" he said carefully, "And he's dead now, then what reason do you have to still be here?"

It was a fair question, one that prompted Cesar to ask it to himself "I suppose that each of us thought the first to leave would seem guilty. We thought it more cautious to remain for the duration."

Turina scowled at him in suspicion "And what? Once he died, you all began to wander around?"

Cesar temporarily lost his focus as he dwelled on this question. As absurd as it sounded, it was exactly what happened.

"Where have I seen you before?" Capaldi said abruptly.

For a few seconds, Cesar thought he was the one being addressed, and his mind worked to come up with the time and place he could've encountered this tall Italian fascist.

"I asked 'Where I have seen you before!?'" he reiterated, and it soon became clear who he was talking to.

"What!?" Von Strichtenheimer exclaimed, looking flustered "Me!?"

"Yes, you! What's your name?"

Von Strichtenheimer's eyes darted back and forth. "I…I'm Felix von Strichtenheimer."

When this name didn't resonate with Capaldi, this appeared to give him reason to doubt. He looked away in thought.

"What's your full name?" Cesar asked.

Capaldi narrowed his eyes at him "Why do you ask?"

"You don't recognize his name, but perhaps he'll recognize yours?" Cesar suggested.

He blinked a few times and glanced at Von Strichtenheimer "I'm Ernesto Capaldi. Have you heard my name before?"

"No," Von Strichtenheimer said quickly. He looked distracted, as if these five men who held him against his will were an inconvenience that kept him from something.

Turina growled, and stared with derision at Cesar and Von Strichtenheimer. "If you two are no use to us, then what do you propose we do with you?"

"Let us be," Von Strichtenheimer suggested earnestly. "We'll go to our rooms and not interfere with you."

They all laughed at this, all apart from Capaldi. He had grown silent since thinking he recognized Von Strichtenheimer.

"How stupid he must think we are," Turina said jovially. "Do you really think we'd take that chance? You could alert Rombauer or the local authorities."

Von Strichtenheimer stared at the carpet in frustration, he was searching for a way out of this. Cesar had the misgiving that he was on the verge of offering to help them hunt down Rombauer. Whatever it took to keep him unharmed and unfettered.

Corvo thoughtfully stroked his chin with the hand that wasn't holding Cesar's revolver. "I wonder if he's an associate of Rombauer. Perhaps his bodyguard?"

Cesar cast a bewildered glance at Corvo, wondering how such a conclusion was reached. Von Strichtenheimer was the most bewildered, looking thoroughly stupefied. "You suspect *what?*" he blurted out.

Even Corvo's compatriots looked skeptical. He grinned good-naturedly as he saw he needed to explain himself.

"Capaldi, you read the same dossiers I did. Rombauer attended a conference in Latvia a few years prior. That's when the Nazis first sent their representatives to approach him, but he had those aggressive bodyguards. They were similar in age to this man, similar in how they dressed. They also had Luger pistols just like him. Are we to assume it's a coincidence?"

It was a coincidence, Cesar thought. There was nothing linking Von Strichtenheimer and Rombauer together, the two of them had barely said a word to each other the entire night. These men were newcomers and were concocting theories based on what little they had.

Capaldi tapped Cesar. "What about this one Corvo?" he asked, breaking his momentary silence. "Who's he?"

Corvo looked at Cesar with indifference. "Oh I don't know, perhaps he really is a private investigator. There's much strange that is going on here. The only possibility that occurs to me is that he's an asset of the Atlantic Powers, the Anglo-Saxons or the

French or the like. We were informed they'd be in the vicinity."

Francis Edmund Dickerson was that asset, and he was guarding Rombauer as they spoke. Once again Cesar knew more than these bastards, and it provided him satisfaction.

Von Strichtenheimer meanwhile, had composed himself enough to state the obvious. "This is circumstantial. I've never met Rombauer before tonight, you have no reason or evidence to believe otherwise."

"Are you not the only two German guests here?" Corvo inquired.

"I'm not German."

"Have you forgotten you told us your name, sir?" Corvo said testily. "Von Stracht-something or Von Stricht-something, it was an obnoxiously Teutonic name. If you are not German, then neither are the Brothers Grimm."

Renzetti and the rodent-faced man sniggered as they continued to restrain an increasingly annoyed Von Strichtenheimer "I'm Teutonic, but not German. I'm an Austro-Hungarian by birth, but I presently live in the Netherlands-"

"You're Austrian?" Capaldi said suddenly, a look of realization illuminating his face.

Von Strichtenheimer was just about to answer that he was, but before he could utter one syllable, he stopped himself and gave the aghast look of a man who said more than he should've. They had all seen the look on his face, he was exposed.

"You were in Spain!" Capaldi declared jubilantly.

Von Strichtenheimer remained frozen like a deer who had heard a predator nearby.

"I didn't know your name, but I knew you were Austrian!"

Capaldi was vehement now, and Von Strichtenheimer's behavior all but confirmed it. Cesar was more than willing to be quiet and let Capaldi extract the relevant information.

"What's going on Capaldi? You know this man!?" Turina said.

"I don't know him intimately, but I met him once in Spain, when I was with the expeditionary force to support the Falangist Revolution."

Cesar was doing his best to seem like he wasn't there. Von Strichtenheimer had fought for the Nationalists in Spain? Just as Galopin and Pryce had fought for the Republicans? What did this mean?

"I've never been to Spain," Von Strichtenheimer said, trying to seem like he was hopelessly confused.

"He's lying," Capaldi announced to his men, stating it as if it were a weather report.

"Why would he lie?" Corvo asked. "What significance is it that you two have met before?"

A pertinent question, Cesar thought.

"This has nothing to do with what we're here for," Turina said, looking and sounding irate.

"Perhaps it does..." Capaldi suggested.

He approached Von Strichtenheimer and grabbed him by the top of his hair, he pulled out a dagger and held it up to younger man's face.

"Tell me about your time in Spain, and then tell me what brought you here tonight." It was a command, but he was genteel about it. "You'll answer these questions, or I'll confiscate one of your ears. If you continue lying, one your eyes will be next." He explained all this like a doctor explaining a procedure to a patient.

Capaldi's men watched this with grim indifference. All except the young blonde Italian named Renzetti, who could barely conceal his glee at the prospect of an imminent atrocity.

Cesar saw the conflict on Von Strichtenheimer's face, his instincts of self-preservation pitted against his iron-willed determination to continue wearing the mask he had been wearing all night.

"If you die here, then it won't be me who kills you," Capaldi said harshly, his patience at an end. "But I won't be deceived by you or anyone else, you have only seconds to decide." This ultimatum didn't extract any confession from Von Strichtenheimer, and the unyielding look on his face suggested he was prepared to sacrifice an ear to carry on with his act.

Cesar decided he wasn't going to stay silent while Von Strichtenheimer was carved up in front of him. He was going to speak up, and he knew just what to say…But then he started to think otherwise, maybe Von Strichtenheimer needed to suffer before he started telling the truth about who he was and what he was doing here. Maybe his ear was the cost of his bullshit.

He thought this up until the point Capaldi brought the blade to Von Strichtenheimer's ear.

"Biassiano's dead!" Cesar shouted.

Chapter 11
Ghosts of Rome

All eyes went to Cesar. Capaldi still held Von Strichtenheimer by the hair and still had the dagger against his face, yet his attention was also focused on Cesar. "What did you say?" he asked coolly, even though he had obviously heard Cesar.

"Biassiano's dead. Someone killed him, just like they killed Decarli."

The "someone" in question was in the room with them. Cesar avoided glancing at Von Strichtenheimer, but he could somehow sense the man looking at him out of the corner of his eye.

"He was found in the wine cellar," Cesar invented. "Someone had stabbed him in the neck." Cesar remembered that he had shot Biassiano "...He also had gunshot wounds," he hastily added.

Capaldi lowered the dagger from Von Strichtenheimer's face, but still held him by the hair. "Why did you lie then?" he asked, pointing at Cesar accusingly with the dagger. "You told us that you didn't know where he was?"

"I thought it better that I didn't get involved, and that the best was to plead ignorance. But I'm not going to sit here and let you hurt this man." Cesar thought about Rombauer, who was still alive, and who he wanted to protect. It was preferrable that he reveal Biassiano's fate, even if it merely bought time.

Capaldi released his grip on Von Strichtenheimer's hair, letting the man fall to the ground. He then immediately placed his foot on Von Strichtenheimer and began addressing his men.

"Corvo, Renzetti. You two will go with this man, and he will take you to Biassiano."

"Do you expect us to bring Biassano's dead body back here?" Corvo asked.

"No, I only want to make sure he's telling the truth. If he's unable to, then it means he's as duplicitous as our Austrian friend. If so, you have my leave to break his legs."

The young blonde Italian named Renzetti gave Cesar such a look of enthusiastic cruelty that he suspected his legs would be broken regardless of what happened.

"However, if he's telling the truth, and Biassiano is dead, then Rombauer is our mission. We find him and make it clear he's coming with us, and then we leave. If possible, a few of us will come back for the prefect's body."

"Turina, you and I will go upstairs to find Rombauer's room." He held up a piece of paper. Cesar wondered what the piece of paper was, but then realized it probably had the room numbers for Biassiano and Rombauer. Either they forced the room numbers from the concierge, or Biassiano had told them during his earlier phone call in the lobby.

"Battaglia, you stay here and watch our Austrian friend."

The rodent-looking man named Battaglia looked at Von Strichtenheimer "Why watch him? Let's just kill him if he's a problem."

Battaglia was the last of the Italians to speak. Cesar wasn't expecting him to have such a posh and melodious voice. It was strange to hear it coming out of his rodent-like face. "You don't want to kill anyone here tonight," Cesar said.

"Oh we don't, do we?"

"Renzetti! I will have you flogged!"

Renzetti closed his mouth and blinked a few times. Capaldi sighed and looked back at Battaglia "I'm not finished with him. If possible, I shall have the truth from him before we depart."

Their orders clear, Capaldi and his men set out. He and Turina went through one door to find the stairs that led upstairs. Corvo and Renzetti took Cesar with them out another door so that he would lead them to Biassiano's body. Battaglia remained in the drawing room with Von Strichtenheimer. The Austrian was made to sit and glower in a chair while Battaglia paced around him with his Luger.

Corvo and Renzetti didn't talk at all as Cesar led them to the kitchen, not to him or to each other. Only Cesar spoke as he muttered directions such as "This way" or "Down here."

This left him to silently worry about Rombauer and Dickerson.

The room they were in was barricaded, and Dickerson had Biassiano's beretta. But that would've only slowed down someone like Capaldi. Maybe the gunshots would attract Galopin, who would prove an even match. For now, he needed to focus on the two of Capaldi's men he was with. Corvo had his LeMat Revolver, and he intended to retrieve it.

As Cesar walked up to the kitchen doors, he heard the voices of the staff back inside. He stopped short of going in. This didn't stop Corvo from marching right the doors, Renzetti grabbed Cesar and escorted him into the kitchen.

The kitchen staff were milling about and socializing as they waited for the night to be over. The arrival of Cesar and two strangers, one of whom was armed, quickly grabbed the staff's attention. Some of them looked frightened, others confused. A large chef with jet black hair and a crooked nose approached them.

"Who are you? The kitchen is–"

He stopped as Corvo pointed the gun at him. Rather than panic, he simply raised his hands in front of him.

"Remain calm, we're not here to hurt you. We've been told there's a body in the wine cellar. We are here to see for ourselves, and then we will go."

The large chef looked towards the wine cellar door where

Pietro Biassiano lay entombed. Cesar recalled that he had watched this man and his colleagues run from the kitchen when Biassiano had taken over the wine cellar to conduct an interrogation of Francis Dickerson. And now they had returned and were certainly aware of Biasiano's dead body downstairs.

Cesar was therefore unsure how this large chef would respond to the situation in front of him. It depended on how much he knew about what was going on tonight, and what orders the Decarlis had given him,

"Are you the gendarmerie?" he asked.

"We're men who don't appreciate being questioned by a cook!" Renzetti spat.

The large chef absorbed the abuse with a look of stone.

"Renzetti a little patience if you will," Corvo chided in a relaxed voice. "It is unimportant who we are, sir," he said to the chef. "We've been instructed to look in the cellar, and that's all we will do."

"I'm afraid we don't just let anyone down there," the chef said, sounding more confident. He asked them if they were the authorities, and they didn't answer the question, which meant they weren't.

Cesar couldn't see Renzetti behind him, but he could hear the indignant and malevolent sounds he was making. If Corvo told him to, he would maim every chef in this kitchen.

Corvo gave no signs he was ready for violence. "I'm attempting to be reasonable, but not because I must be," he said mellowly. "I will ask only once more for you to kindly let us into the cellar, or else I will have to be unreasonable; I think."

Cesar had been waiting for the best moment to strike. He eyed a glass bottle on the counter to the left of him and settled on acting once the large chef had responded to Corvo's threat.

"Then you will have to be unreasonable, I think," the chef answered, mocking the way Corvo talked.

Cesar grabbed the glass bottle with his left hand and swung it behind him in the direction of Renzetti's head. He expected the bottle to shatter against him, but it instead remained intact as it slammed into the skull. Cesar thought he heard a cracking noise, and then Renzetti fell to the ground.

Corvo spun around, the LeMat Revolver still in his hand. Cesar dropped the bottle and grabbed onto the gun. Their struggle was brief, as the kitchen staff to swarm them, armed with knives and cleavers. Corvo lost his grip on the gun as he was overtaken by the swarm of chefs.

Now back in control of his gun, Cesar jumped out of the way, almost tripping over Renzetti as he did so. He then watched in disbelief as the chefs stabbed Corvo with their knives, Corvo tried to shout, but was only able to croak as he was repeatedly stabbed.

Cesar tore his eyes away from the gruesome sight, and pointed his revolver at where Renzetti was on the ground. "Stay where you are!"

Renzetti didn't seem to hear Cesar, he climbed up off the ground, looking disoriented and bleeding from the head.

"I said stay where you are!"

Renzetti looked at Cesar as if he had just noticed him. His eyes were bright with anger, showing that thoughts of hostility still lurked in his possibly injured brain. He took a foreboding step forward, which was all Cesar needed to shoot him in the shoulder. Renzetti staggered backwards, but remained standing, his teeth gritted in pain.

The large chef, who was now covered in Corvo's blood, approached Renzetti from behind and stuck him in the back with his blade. Renzetti's face, once so full of sadism, was now covered in shock. For a few seconds, he momentarily locked eyes with Cesar as if to audaciously plead for help.

Two of the chefs grabbed Renzetti and carried him off. Another one was dragging away the already dead Corvo, the trail of blood marking the floor as he went. The large chef remained standing where he was, his white uniform stained with red and the knife dangling from his hand.

"We'll throw them in the cellar with the other one," he said strictly, sounding like a soldier giving a report. "If I were you, I'd fuck off out of our kitchen."

Cesar, speechless and in shock about what had just happened, forced himself to turn around and walk out the kitchen door. He stood in the corridor for a few moments, and for a few strange moments it was almost like he forgot where he was and what he was doing…and then reality came flooding back.

Rombauer and Dickerson, upstairs. He took off running down the halls, determined to find the nearest stairwell. His run slowed to a walk as he came to a hallway he recognized; he stopped walking to consult the hotel map – He froze at the sight of Ernesto Capaldi rounding the corner towards him. Any thought of hiding from Capaldi disappeared when the man's eagle-like eyes locked onto Cesar.

Cesar pulled out his revolver, looking away from Capaldi as he did so. When he looked back up, Capaldi was charging up to him. He slapped the gun out of Cesar's hand, and it tumbled along the floor. Capaldi's hands were then around Cesar's neck, he lifted him off the ground.

Cesar attempted to speak through the suffocation but could only sputter. Capaldi wasn't listening and instead looked at a wooden door that led to an undisclosed room. Suddenly he was dropped to the ground.

Cesar got to his knees and caught his breath, there was no sense in running from Capaldi, nor in grabbing his revolver, he was now this man's hostage.

Capaldi opened the door, forced Cesar to his feet and shoved him into the room whose door he had just opened. Cesar looked around the room, it was some sort of gallery filled with suits of armor and glass display cases.

"What was that gunshot?" Capaldi said with a slam of the door.

"It was my gun," Cesar told the truth. Now it was time for the lie "I tried to wrestle it away from your man, but it went off."

"You're lying," Capaldi said dourly, almost sounding sad.

Cesar sought to distract him with a question of his own "What have you done to Rombauer?"

"Nothing. We found his room, but we couldn't get in. A man on the other side of the door threatened us and said to go away, but I don't think it was Rombauer. He sounded American."

Dickerson had followed Cesar's instructions and barricaded Rombauer's room, and he was diligently defending the much sought after engineer. The old American was more reliable than he looked.

"Tell me what that gunshot was!" Capaldi said energetically, taking firm control of the conversation.

"I've already said it was my gun-"

"My men aren't with you, and you have the gun they took from you. That means it was likely you shot them."

Capaldi was an intelligent man, Lying or not answering would've had devasting consequences.

"Yes, they're dead," Cesar said, wishing he could somehow take the words back after having said them. He tried to not pay much attention to the feeling of impending doom.

"And you killed them?" Capaldi said, his voice and temperament inexplicably mild. It would've been less terrifying if he started screaming at him.

Cesar felt himself quiver internally, but kept going "I shot one of them, and that was what you heard, but they were killed by others."

"What others?" Capaldi demanded.

"The hotel chefs."

Capaldi stared at him a few moments before responding "What!?"

     An Event in Luxembourg

"The men who work in the hotel kitchen killed your men!" Cesar said impatiently. The kitchen staff demonstrated they could defend themselves, so he wasn't overly worried about them and their wellbeing.

Capaldi regarded Cesar with a ponderous, scrutinizing expression. He then abruptly grabbed Cesar and threw him up against the door to the corridor.

Cesar turned around so his back was against the door, and held his hands defensively out in front of him "What are you…"

"I'm taking you Rombauer's room. I have hope that the sounds of your screaming will be able to persuade the men inside to come out." Capaldi said with unenthusiastic severity. If it was possible to respectfully tell someone you were going to torture them, then he had come close to doing so.

The prospect that he would endure agonizing pain to bring Dickerson and Rombauer out of hiding was one of such enormity that he was unable to process fear of it. He instead felt the urgent need to avert this undesirable occurrence.

"I may have a better idea…" Cesar began to say, wondering himself what that idea was.

"Lead the way!" Capaldi yelled.

Cesar took a breath to steady himself, and then opened the door, but someone was already standing there…And that was someone was Major Dieudonne Galopin, who had his arms crossed and an aloof expression. He didn't look at Cesar, instead looking over Cesar's shoulder at Capaldi, his mouth turning into a sneer.

Cesar could scarcely remember the last time he was so pleased to see someone. He stood out of the way and let Galopin into the room. Capaldi said nothing as the angry Frenchman marched towards him, but the agitated look on his face said it all.

The minute Galopin was within striking distance, Capaldi struck him across the face with an enclosed fist. Galopin absorbed it as if someone had gently slapped him, and then plowed into Capaldi with full force.

Cesar went out into the corridor to retrieve his revolver and then rushed back into the room. He arrived just in time to see Capaldi throw Galopin into a suit of armor, which broke around him.

"Don't move! I'll shoot you!" he announced, aiming at Capaldi.

Capaldi and Galopin continued fighting as if he wasn't there.

"I'm armed!" he said a little louder than before.

Neither man so much as looked at him.

Realizing he was a bystander; Cesar rested against the wall and watched the fight. He would intervene only if he needed to.

Galopin and Capaldi were in their fifties, both fought in the Great War, and both were far more dangerous than the average individual. The advantage went to Galopin though, who was more strongly built than the tall and skinny Capaldi, and who was likely the fiercer one by a slim margin.

After half a minute of fighting, Galopin found a way to end the fight. He picked up the spear from the suit of armor they broke and hit Capaldi across the face with it. As his opponent hit the ground, Galopin then raised the spear in the air and pierced him through the leg with it.

Capaldi didn't shout, but instead made a hissing, seething noise. Cesar watched all this in silent awe.

Galopin wiped his brow with his hand, keeping his other hand on the spear. "I don't want to prolong your suffering, so answer my questions in a timely manner," he said in a calm, conversational voice. "What's your name?"

"Ernesto Capaldi," he answered through gritted teeth.

"And what are you doing here?"

"I am here to assist Pietro Biassiano in drafting Ludwig Rombauer into service to the Italian-German alliance, and to complete his objective should he be unable to."

"Is it just you?"

Cesar answered "There are four others, two are dead. One's in the drawing room with Von Strichtenheimer. I don't know where the other one is."

"I left Turina to stand watch at Rombauer's room," Capaldi said.

Galopin narrowed his eyes in disapproval as he gazed down at Capaldi "We're not far from the German border. I presume that's where you were heading once you had Rombauer?"

"Yes."

"You leave him with his Nazi captors so he can build them weapons, then you go back across the Alps and your potentate in Rome pats you on the head for being a good little fascist."

"It is not the worst that I've done."

Galopin bared his teeth like they were fangs "I have no doubt of that…Where else have you served? In Africa, where you used mustard gas against the Abyssinians? In Albania, where you bravely conquered peasant villages? In Spain, where you made war against a people who were already at war with each other?"

Capaldi scowled up at the man who bested him, glinting indignation in his eyes "I noticed you are French. How is what your people did in Algeria different than what mine are doing now?"

Rather than become hostile or defensive, Galopin looked pained. As if he had been reminded of an unpleasant memory or a childhood friend that died.

"It is the way of men that great nations are responsible for great deeds and great sins," he lamented in a distant voice. "There are times I suspect the last war was cosmic punishment: For Europe and our idiotic empires, for the Russians and the Turks and their empires."

Cesar sensed that Galopin was just as much talking to himself as he was Capaldi.

"I serve the Italians and their King, His Majesty Victor

Emmanuel III," Capaldi growled, a look of stalwart conviction on his face. "This decaying world needs salvation, it needs civilization, it needs Rome! Even if it comes at the expense of those who choose to resist it!" He had said all this with an energetic frenzy that proved his worth as a fascist, the spear that was embedded in him but an inconvenience.

Now wore out from his exertion, Capaldi lay his head down on the floor with a blissful look on his face. He was aware he wouldn't be raising his head ever again. "…I've learned not to make it more complicated than that."

Galopin peered down at Capaldi with a look of what could be described as unwilling camaraderie. "I too have done my country's will when it wasn't right. In this instance though, the forces of fate and providence didn't impart their mark on you. I am sorry your death was not more important, but at least you will die violently as a Roman should. I hope God treats you fairly."

"I don't believe in God," Capaldi said gently.

Galopin merely nodded at him. "If He is real, then tell him that it was *La Pendu de Verdun* who sent you."

The French soldier than took on the look of a man who was about to perform an execution. He grasped his hands around the spear, raised his right foot and stomped it down onto Capaldi's head, he did this two times more. Each stomp was accompanied by a ghastly sound that Cesar understood to be the sound of the man's head breaking open.

Galopin was a hardened man, but he wasn't a vile or unscrupulous man. In that moment though, as he used his boot to destroy a man's head, Galopin had a look in his eyes that was more unnerving than anything Cesar had seen that night. It was a look that Cesar had seen before, a look that he had described to others: Some of whom had also seen the look before…They had come to call it "A look not explained by reason."

The look on Galopin's face was gone as quickly as it appeared.

His face was now made of stone, yet his eyes were on fire. He scanned the room, looking like a man who had forgotten where he was.

He jerked his head Cesar's direction. The fire fading from his eyes as reality seemed to be settling back in. He cleared his throat before speaking, and when he did speak it was with uncharacteristic tranquility "I will deal with the man in the drawing room, you should see to the man outside Rombauer's room."

Cesar sensed he didn't have much of a choice, but he had been heading there regardless. "I'll meet you in the drawing room once I'm done."

Galopin nodded wordlessly, and they left.

Cesar knew the way to Rombauer's room without the use of the map. He had spent enough time running around this hotel to be familiar enough with its layout. Once he was gone, he'd gladly remember as little as possible.

Four gunshots rang out. "Jesus Christ," Cesar said as he picked up the pace.

When he arrived outside Rombauer's room, he saw Turina slumped up against the wall adjacent to the door. He strolled up to the injured thug, observing the four bullet holes in Rombauer's room as he did so.

"Get away!" Turina snarled at the sight of an approaching Cesar. "Capaldi will-"

"Capaldi's dead," Cesar said morbidly, "and so are two of the remaining three."

Turina didn't react immediately, his ugly mug blankly contemplating what he had just heard. He then broke out into a furious grimace "Vaffanculo! I'll see you in hell you fuck-"

Cesar raised his revolver and blasted a hole in Turina's chest, near where his heart was. His head hit the back of the corridor wall, he made a few guttural sounds and then he was quiet.

He turned towards the door. "Dickerson?"

"Who's there now!?" Dickerson's voice said.

"It's Mondragon, sir."

"Did you kill him?"

"I did, yes," Cesar said, neither proud or ashamed of it. "I presume you're the one who shot him first?"

"The bastard outside was trying to break in and making all sorts of horrific threats. Who the hell are these people?"

"Friends of Pietro Biassiano."

The American government man could be heard making indignant noises "The intelligence said Biassiano would be in Luxembourg alone...You can be sure that's going in my report!"

"How's Rombauer?"

"A nervous wreck, but otherwise fine."

"Good..." Cesar said, taking a breath. "You should probably stay put for the time being."

"Oh, I think we rather like it in here."

Cesar went back downstairs, fervently praying he wouldn't hear anymore gunshots. He opened the doors to the drawing room, wondering what he'd find...Galopin was standing in there alone.

Where had Von Strichtenheimer and his captor gone?

He approached Galopin "Major, what..."

Cesar stopped as he saw what the Frenchman was looking at: Battaglia, the rodent faced Blackshirt, lay on the ground with his neck broken.

"Did you kill him?" Cesar said instantly.

"I found him this way," Galopin said. He was neither looking at Cesar or the body on the ground, but was instead vigilantly watching the various entrances to the drawing room.

"Von Strichtenheimer..." Cesar determined. "It must've been."

"Yes, most likely...I heard more gunshots, so I trust the other one is also dead?"

"All five jackboots have been accounted for."

"And Biassiano makes six in all, six ghosts of Rome."

"Ghosts of Rome?" Cesar asked.

Now Galopin was looking at him. "Mussolini wants his soldiers and militants to be like the Legions of Rome, he wants to reforge the power balance of the antiquity, when the Mediterranean was an Italian lake."

"But he isn't a Roman Emperor, he's the Prime Minister of Italy. And he doesn't command the Legions of Rome, he commands the Royal Italian Armed Forces and an auxiliary force of ruffians dressed in black."

"He thinks he's Caesar, but he's opportunistic lout wearing a fez…It is you who is Cesar."

He laughed softly at Galopin's stupid joke, it felt good to laugh.

"These men though? My evaluation is that they succeeded. By dying so violently for their cause, they showed themselves worthy of the title of Roman, a distinction they fell short of in life. And now they're united with the other Ghosts of Rome."

A poignant pause followed. And then the drawing room clock struck three times.

"It's three," Galopin said. "I thought it was closer to sunrise."

"Yes, so did I," Cesar said. Time seemed to work differently when he was the thick of it. He knew that exhaustion would come sooner or later, once there was no more chaos for him to feed off of.

"This has been one of the longer nights of my life."

Cesar suddenly thought Galopin looked old, old and…worn out. It was easy to disregard how old he really was when he normally emanated such strength and fortitude.

"At least Kenneth is resting," Galopin said earnestly. "It has simplified things and lifted a burden now that I no longer have to worry about him."

The mention of the murdered Kenneth Pryce put Cesar in a state of alert. A few hours prior, Galopin had been aghast to learn of Pryce's death. And he had been hostile when Cesar began to share his knowledge of their friendship and the nebulous job Alexander Decarli had hired them for.

Now he sounded relaxed and untroubled as he talked about his friend who was "resting." It had "simplified things" and "lifted a burdened."

Cesar thought about all the comrades Galopin had lost, in the Great War, in Spain, and in any other war he'd been in. And then Cesar thought about himself and the friends he lost…He thought about those he still had and where they were now.

The two men looked at each other, awkwardly aware of the moment they were experiencing. "Von Strichtenheimer is unaccounted for," Galopin said, his voice had returned to its usual steely timbre. "I will go and search for him…Can I trust you to search for Decarli's daughter?"

Cesar was about to say he had no idea where she was, but then he noticed the painting on the wall above them. The same painting he had used to look into the drawing room from the passageways. And then it suddenly became obvious to him where Valencia Decarli was. "I…I actually think I know precisely where to find her."

"Indeed?" Galopin said. He glanced briefly at the painting, looking curious. "…Let's get on with it, then?"

Cesar left the drawing room again.

An Event in Luxembourg

ACT

IV

Chapter 12
Valencia's Tale

Cesar searched the passageways for several long minutes, before eventually stumbling upon the familiar staircase that led up to the subterranean room he had discovered earlier. The door was unlocked this time, and he let himself him.

Valencia sat in one of the chairs at the circular table that took up one end of the room. She had prepared herself tea, making use of the tea set and stove.

"Ah Cesar, here we are at the witching hour," Her tone was perfectly pleasant. "Would you like some tea?"

He took a seat in the chair opposite hers. "What I would like is for you to make sense out of all these occurrences."

"What occurrences are those?"

"Your father and his machinations, his murder, Melikov and Von Strichtenheimer, Galopin and Pryce and the job they were hired for. And I've found out recently of Dickerson's employment with the U.S. State Department, and his intent to protect Doctor Rohmbauer from hostile powers This is all interconnected somehow, they are part of a greater event that has happened tonight. Now is the time for you to help make sense of that event."

She gave a brief nod to indicate that she understood "What do you most want to know?"

"I want to know why Felix von Strichtenheimer killed your father."

She smiled at him "Bravo, I was not free from doubt when I said that you knew who killed him, but it is good to see that my trust in your capabilities was not misplaced."

"I believe that he killed Pryce as well."

Valencia seemed moderately surprised "What makes you certain of that?"

"When I followed him on the floor, he disappeared after turning into a dead-end corridor. Not long after that, I found Pryce dead in his room and an entrance to the passageways in his wardrobe. Therefore, the best explanation I can produce is that Von Strichtenheimer knew about the secret passageways, accessed them from the third-floor corridor, and used them to ambush Pryce in his room."

"How do you think he knew about the passageways?" Valencia asked, a slight tone of unease in her voice. This had the appearance of a genuine question about something that she did not know.

Until now, Cesar had no thought of how Von Strichtenheimer knew of the existence of the passageways. Thankfully, answers soon came to him. "Either he happened to find them like I did, or he somehow knew about them beforehand. As to how he possibly knew about them beforehand, I lack a sufficient answer."

"I see...More importantly, do you know why he would kill Pryce?"

"Pryce most likely killed Melikov, so that may be a part of it," Cesar said, feeling dumb for answering because Valencia almost absolutely knew the answer herself.

"I also encountered Von Strichtenheimer when we both thought to trespass in Galopin's room. He attempted to throw me off guard with a concocted story of Galopin and Pryce being the guilty parties."

"Oh yes?" she asked, once again sounding strangely pleasant.

"His theory was mildly convincing, if not amateurishly assembled. Unfortunately for him, I had vital information that contradicted that theory and instead exposed him as the guilty party. You and your father's written messages to each other refer to a single 'him' who serves as the purpose of the event that has been held here. Von Strichtenheimer told me otherwise. He said that the purpose of the event was two or three men, which would've made these messages incoherent."

"I didn't assume you and your father were lying to each other, and since I already had suspicions of him. It was apparent that Von Strichtenheimer was misleading me and that he was the nameless 'him.' And as we learned from Doctor Gounelle, your father was poisoned forty-five minutes before he died,"

Cesar paused dramatically. "The individual he met with forty-five minutes prior was Felix von Strichtenheimer."

Valencia was quiet after Cesar finished and stared into her tea "Were you fully aware of all these details as Von Strichtenheimer told you?"

"For the most part, yes."

"Then why not dispatch him then and there?" she asked, sounding disappointed.

Cesar's mind turned to the five dead Italian fascists upstairs. "We we're distracted."

Valencia looked faintly worried by this cryptic remark "Distracted by what?"

She didn't know? Very well then, he'd tell her.

"Biassiano brought a support team with him to Luxembourg. They evidently thought he was taking too long to knab Rombauer, so they stormed the hotel looking for them both. They were dispatched by the combined forces of myself, Von Strichtenheimer, Galopin, Dickerson, and the gentlemen employed in your kitchen."

Valencia listened to this insane turn of events with such a detached and moderate look, that Cesar couldn't tell how cognizant she had been of any of it. "I recall hearing strange noises," she said, before taking a drink from her tea.

"Did I assume correctly?" he pressed. "Is Von Strichtenheimer the 'he' that you and your father referred to in your messages to each other?"

She closed her eyes "He is."

"Tell me everything. Why he killed your father, why the two of you were interested in him. No more secrets Valencia."

She opened her eyes back up "It is not a question I can answer briefly. If you really must know everything, then I have a story to tell you."

"Then begin."

She was quiet for a long time, leaving them sitting in the loud silence that filled the room. The world outside of this room was not so quiet, as the major powers were in crisis and another global conflict seemed imminent. But all was peaceful in the room that Cesar and Valencia currently occupied, and there was nothing imminent apart from the story she would be telling.

"My mother was not like my father. He was the son of merchants and profiteers. She was of prominent birth. Her father was a French nobleman who came from a cadet branch of the House of Normandy, their family lost nearly everything during the French Revolution and spent the next one-hundred-and-twenty years reclaiming all that they could. Her mother was an educated German who belonged to a series of interrelated families that had belonged to the lower nobility of the Holy Roman Empire. They met at one of his parties in Switzerland in 1908, he was twenty-five and she was twenty-two. It was not love at first sight or anything so fantastical, they knew each other for two years before a relationship blossomed between them."

"They spent a year together in Switzerland and Northern Italy, March 1911 to March 1912. It was during this period that she became pregnant and did not care to notify her family in France, who she was on poor terms with. Nobody who saw her pregnant knew her, and therefore she was able to keep it a secret. My father respected her wishes and did not inform his family and friends. I was born in early February of 1912 in a town on the shores of Lake Geneva. The two of them never told me what town it was, and I rather like the idea of it being a mystery."

"That summer she was summoned back to France by her own father. He was an authoritarian and medieval man who took issue with her being nearly twenty-seven and still not having a husband. In the time that she had been away, he had arranged for her to be married to a family of the Austrian nobility."

The sheer weight of what she said took a moment to register with him. "A family of the Austrian nobility...You can't seriously mean..."

"She was to marry Siegfried von Strichtenheimer, and her father had put her in such a position that she could not back out of the marriage. My mother informed my father of what she was being forced to do; and him being the man he was, acted immediately. He prepared a plan to have the engagement ruined and my mother freed from her obligation."

"The plan involved in another Austrian family named the Peithners, my father was connected to them through his business arrangements, they were an independently wealthy family who were outside the nobility and therefore were looked down upon by the Von Strichtenheimers. Father persuaded a few of the Peithners to propagate rumors of my mother's affair with a Swiss commoner and having a child out of wedlock, rumors which were obviously true, but of course my father knew better then to give the Peithners evidence to verify their claims. He understood the nobility well enough to know that the rumors alone would've been enough to sabotage the wedding...But what my father did not anticipate how the Von Strichtenheimers would react."

"Siegfried von Strichtenheimer, along with his younger brother Baldur, angrily denounced the Peithners and accused them of slandering their family. At my father's encouragement, the Peithers remained steadfast in their allegations and many in the Austrian aristocracy started to believe the rumors about my mother. Siegfried's father called off the engagement, my mother's father also believed the rumors and disowned her. My mother was devastated at being abandoned by her family, but she was also free to be with my father and the daughter they had created."

She smiled softly and touched her chin as she thought about her parents. This only lasted a few moments before the smile faded and she became sober again. "There is little that I would like more, than to tell you that that was the end of it, but as the happenings of tonight have demonstrated, it was only the beginning of a more unpleasant story."

"Siegfried von Strichtenheimer was furious and believed he had been cheated out of marrying my mother, he along with his brother Baldur and two of their cousins abducted Herbert Peithner, who had played a key role in the rumors. Siegfried attempted to intimidate him into not only confessing that the rumors were false, but to spread this confession throughout the proper social circles. I think Siegfried genuinely believed that he was in love with my mother, as this seemed like a bold attempt to regain the engagement he had with her, it was so bold that he ended up beating Herbert Peithner to death. His body was found in the streets of a slum, a clumsy attempt to make it appear as if was the unfortunate victim of some murderer or thief, but it was clear to everyone who killed Herbert Peithner. Not a week had gone by when a family friend of the Von Strichtenheimers disappeared and was soon found floating in the Danube in Vienna."

"As you can imagine, the situation grew in its severity until one day when it inevitably went too far. In the Fall of 1913, the entire Von Strichtenheimer family attended a formal party where much of the Austrian elite was represented. Several of the Peithners knew that the Von Strichtenheimers would be there and made the terrible and rash mistake of gatecrashing the party. There was much shouting between the two families, and it was soon followed by brawling. Attempts by interlopers to stop the fight only made the situation worse, and soon the brawling was not limited to the Von Strichtenheimers and the Peithners. A man was thrown through a window, a church official was accidently stabbed, someone had brought a pistol with them and it went off. Eventually the party guests were forced to flee from the uncontrollable violence, in the process a woman was trampled to death. By the end of it, dozens had been injured, three were hospitalized, and a young woman was dead."

"The event was a shock and a humiliation to the Austrian nobility, nothing of such a horrid nature had occurred since the Mayerling affair in 1889."

"I had associates of mine research the entire guest list," Cesar said. "A scandal involving Von Strichtenheimer's family was mentioned, but there was nothing to indicate what you've described."

Valencia nodded "They did their best to bury it: People were bought off, the state censored newspapers. The obituary of the woman who died said she was run over by a carriage. Your associates probably uncovered enough traces of it to suspect that something bad happened, but little more than that."

"My father understood well that he could not be connected to it and cut all ties with the Peithners, they had been very useful to him in getting my mother out of an unwilling engagement, but they were ultimately expendable."

"The Peithner family received most of the punishment for what happened at the party, not because they were necessarily more at fault, but because they were of a lower social status. The police arrested several of them on smuggling charges. It was an open secret that the Peithners were smugglers, but it was only after the disaster at the party that any action was taken."

"The Von Strichtenheimers suffered consequences as well, but not in the way the Peithners did, their suffering was of their reputation. First, they almost married their favorite son Siegfried to a woman who had allegedly given birth to a child out of wedlock. Then Siegfried, his brother Baldur, and their cousins lowered themselves by engaging in a petty squabble with a lowly family like the Peithners. But it was the disaster that took place at the party that was the worst of all, to have displayed such behavior, and possibly caused the death of an innocent woman? The name Von Strichtenheimer became a pariah to the rest of the Austrian nobility, they were as disreputable as they could be while still retaining their own status. It brought no end of shame and frustration to them."

"One year later, Archduke Franz Ferdinand was assassinated in Sarajevo by the Black Hand. A declaration of war by Austria-Hungary against Serbia followed, as did several more declarations of war by the allies of both nations…I think you know what happened after that."

"The Great War caused the downfall of Austria-Hungary empire and it's nobility," Cesar said.

"The Von Strichtenheimers did not foresee such events when the war started. Many of the military age men in the family saw the war as an opportunity to gain back their family's reputation. The ones who were not already members of the military quickly joined."

"But the war only brought greater pain to the Von Strichtenheimer family. Fourteen sons of the Von Strichtenheimers and their extended family fought in the Great War, but only two survived. It was partially their own doing, as they often put themselves in harm's way in misguided acts of daring, but it also didn't help that their commanding officers enjoyed placing them in situations they could not hope to survive. The greatest loss of all came at the end of the war. Siegfried and Baldur von Strichtenheimer were both captured by Italian forces during the Battle of Vittorio Veneto. If they had been expecting special treatment due to their status, then they did not receive it, an Italian lieutenant shot each of them."

"The Von Strichtenheimers thought the war would be their family's redemption, but it only provided a convenient mechanism for Austrian society to be rid of as many of them as they could. By the time the war ended, the surviving Von Strichtenheimers were nearly all women, children, and older men. There was a giant hole in their family where an entire generation of young men should've been..." She looked like she wanted to say more, but stopped as she seemed to decide that what she already said was suitable.

"One of those children was Felix von Strichtenheimer" Cesar concluded calmly.

"Yes…Siegfried and Baldur were his two older brothers. He was too young to fight in the war, but not too young to remember their funerals, the funerals of many other male relatives, and all the damage it caused to his family. He along with his sisters and mother relocated to the Netherlands shortly after the abolition of the Austrian nobility, and in 1923 he began his education at Oxford."

"From what my father and I were able to find out. During his first year at Oxford, another Austrian who had been attending university in London was found murdered in the building he lived in. He had been the son of a left-wing politician in Austria who had play a vital role in the passing of laws that abolished the nobility. The police never caught the killer."

"You think it was Felix Von Strichtenheimer? The same one here tonight?" Cesar asked.

"Father wasn't entirely sure, but it would fit perfectly. We do know that after graduation, Felix began to travel Europe under assumed names and identities. His mother and sisters kept up the illusion that he was still at their home in the Netherlands. This way, everyone thought that he had resigned himself to a hermitic and scholarly life when he was actually traveling abroad."

"He made his way to Austria where he affiliated himself with Austrian nationalist groups using one of his false identities. Father was very certain that he used the connections he made in

Austria to kill individuals that were somehow part of his family's ruination."

"Three members of the Peither family turned up dead, and it was assumed it had something to do with their smuggling connections. And there was also a retired officer that had sent one of Felix's cousins to his death while at the Romanian front. The officer was murdered while he slept, and his Slovenian nurse was convicted of the crime. The nurse had a sick son, and her family came into a large sum of money after her confession. The police suspected something strange, but there was no further investigation."

"We also believe Felix Von Strichtenheimer was present for the February Uprising in 1934, during which Austria's nationalist government and its supporters' clashed with their communist and socialist opponents. Hundreds of Austrian socialists were killed during this event, and my father had an informant who promised that Von Strichtenheimer took part in those killings."

"He next fought in the Spanish Civil War for a pro-nationalist group. While there he killed upwards of twenty fighters of the Republican forces and gained a hated reputation among them. He was forced to leave Spain in 1938, after the Nationalists suspected him of killing an Italian officer."

"That was fourteen months ago, after that he no longer fraternized with any political or paramilitary groups. He openly despised Mussolini and the Blackshirts in Italy, and the annexation of Austria by Nazi Germany had infuriated him. I suppose that it just came to the point that he little use for them anymore."

"Father and I had kept track on him for a while, we were curious of him and wanted to see what he would do. We were concerned that he would become aware of us, my father was the man who had ruined the engagement between his brother Siegfried and my mother, and I am the product of this love affair. He had killed in retribution for his family before. It was not hard to foresee that he could do it again."

Valencia paused and looked at Cesar with a distressed and pained look. Before he could inquire, she continued. "And then something happened last winter that confirmed our fears and convinced us to take action. My mother had an aunt she was close to, one who lived in Strasbourg. Last December she was murdered by an unknown assailant who invaded her home."

"You think it was Von Strichtenheimer?"

"We suspected it, and then we were able to confirm it. There was a witness who refused to talk to the police but was willing to talk to a representative of my father. They described a man in the area that matched Felix von Strichtenheimer's description. The only reason he would have to kill her was because she was related to my mother. If he was willing to kill my aunt for simply being a relative of the woman who was engaged to his brother. Then we also knew that he would eventually come to kill the two of us."

"My father was prepared to die, but he refused to let Von Strichtenheimer kill me. We immediately crafted a plan. We were going to have Felix von Strichtenheimer killed, and it was going to be on our terms and not his."

"The first step was to find someone who could be trusted to kill him. Father quickly suggested Dieudonne Galopin as the perfect candidate, the two of them had met when my father was selling weapons to the Republicans in Spain. His opinion of Galopin was that he was reliable and pragmatic, yet fierce and passionate. Galopin knew of an unidentified Austrian man fighting for the Nationalists in Spain, one who killed a friend of his. Father of course knew who that man was and offered to give Galopin the opportunity to kill him. A proposition that Galopin was very enthusiastic about."

"We originally considered sending Galopin to hunt down Von Strichtenheimer, but it seemed too crude and simple, and we did not want to risk alerting Von Strichtenheimer to the fact that he was being targeted. We then thought to lure Von Strichtenheimer somewhere where Galopin would be waiting for him, but again we thought it was too risky and Von Strichtenheimer too smart. But then father had an idea that I at first thought was insanity: What if he were to invite Von Strichtenheimer to come to a party, and to make it plain that it was Alexander Decarli that was inviting him?"

"I didn't like it, but there was a cleverness to it. To openly engage Von Strichtenheimer and invite him to come near us. He would be suspicious, but also curious, and that would be enough to convince him to attend our function. Galopin would be hiding in plain sight among the party guests and would kill him when the opportunity arose."

"We contacted the Von Strichtenheimer household to inquire about whether or not Felix would be our guest at a future party. His response surprised both of us, he only wished to attend if he could bring a guest of his own, a Russian accountant living in Copenhagen."

"Melikov," Cesar said.

"Yes, I believe he understood that my father was luring him into a trap, so he hired a man he knew to be former Tsarist secret policeman and killer-for-hire to be his guest at the party. This way Melikov would be caught in the trap if it was sprung, or if Von Strichtenheimer was the victim of the trap as intended, then Melikov would still kill my father."

"My father knew Melikov was not just an accountant, and that he was Von Strichtenheimer's second. He advised Galopin to find a second of his own should he be killed, Pryce was quickly brought up and we had our fourth guest. But then Von Strichtenheimer suddenly informed our representative that he changed his mind about attending the party, possibly he doubted his own ability to outsmart my father."

"My father was prepared for that though and informed Von Strichtenheimer that there would be another guest at the party. A prefect of Italy named Pietro Biassiano, a man who both my father and Von Strichtenheimer were aware of as the Italian lieutenant who executed Siegfried and Baldur Von Strichtenheimer during the war. The chance of killing both my father and the Italian veteran who executed his elder brothers was far too desirable to forgo."

"Biassiano did not wish to attend the party either though. Fortunately, my father was prepared for that as well, he knew from a confidential source in the Italian embassy in Switzerland that Pietro Biassiano was part of a commission of Nazis and Italian Fascists whose objective was to recruit important scientists from neutral nations. Doctor Ludwig Rohmbauer was one of these scientists, a weapons designer from the last war who was sought after by the west along with Hitler and Mussolini. Therefore, we would invite Doctor Rohmbauer as our sixth guest."

"Although this proved another dilemma, my father knew he could not have Doctor Rohmbauer and a member of this German-Italian task force both attend this party without provoking action by the western intelligence services. He contacted certain men in London, Paris, and Washington D.C. and told them of his plans. An arrangement was made for a representative of the west to attend the party as an invited guest, an American businessman who was also an operative for the U.S. State Department."

"Dickerson..." Cesar mused. "That just leaves myself, what am I doing here?"

"Dickerson was supposed to be the final guest, but at that point father realized that the entire plan had become overcomplicated, and he was worried that it would fall apart. I suggested that for our eighth and last guest, we invite a type of trouble-buster. A person who was intelligent, capable, upright, and had a reputation for unraveling complex occurrences. If everything went completely and terribly wrong, then at the very least we could rely on this final guest to make things as right as they could be. We had a few candidates, but we ended up choosing you."

Valencia finished her story and looked at Cesar as if she wanted nothing more than to hear what he thought.

"That's what this has been?" he asked skeptically "An elaborate plot to get rid of Felix von Strichtenheimer?"

"My father believed in being complicated in everything he did, it prevented others from figuring out what he was up to. And as he long as he knew what he was doing, and he very seldom didn't, then little could go wrong."

Cesar thought about what other unanswered questions he had "He said at dinner he was dying, I assume this was also part of your ruse?"

"His liver wasn't in the most enviable of conditions, unsurprising since he discovered his love for liquor at the age of twelve. His heart was also beginning to give us reason to worry, a defect he inherited from his father's side of the family.

"And I'll confess he was uncertain about the prospect of his longevity. He'd have turned fifty-seven the next year, the same age his father – my paternal grandfather – was when his heart gave out. Apart from that, he didn't suffer from anything terminal. His proclamation of imminent death was apocryphal."

Valencia stopped talking, and for a few moments Cesar thought he was supposed to say something, but then she continued, "Ever since mother died, he had a longing desire to join her…He didn't though… He had me to raise me, he had people and responsibilities to see to."

A melancholic look came across her face, one that was both sorrowful and joyous. Eventually the joy seemed to win over and she had a radiant smile. It was the sincerest look Cesar had seen from her all night. "And he did so wonderfully for twenty years," she said with reverence for her late father.

"Once he and I concocted his scheme, and the question of him dying presented itself…"

She paused, a hesitant look of conflict and guilt about her. "I gave him permission…To make his exit, in a manner of speaking," she finished quickly, before drinking from her tea again.

Cesar then thought about where it all began for him, about the gangster from Marseilles and the first time he heard Alexander Decarli's name. "Valencia, do you have any recollection of a man named Antonin Rocca?"

She thought and shook her head "No…No, I can't say that name resonates…Please, tell me about him."

"He was a gangster in Corsica, one that I met two years ago. Rocca was hired to commit a murder that cost him more than he imagined. I was sent to track him down, and he told me about the man who hired him…He said it was your father."

Cesar paused, having some vague idea that Valencia would immediately deny her father's involvement in hiring common thugs to commit miscellaneous murders. Either that or to confirm he had done it as if it were a typical transaction. She instead regarded him with a raised eyebrow, so he went on.

"I didn't think much of it, but then Rocca was found dead in his prison cell. Therefore, I investigated the matter further, but there was nothing for me to investigate. I spoke to some shady characters in Venice who were unwilling to talk to me, and I heard about another person in Switzerland who pulled a disappearing act."

All this talk of people her father more than likely had killed, and the fear other living people had of him, seemed to affect her. She wasn't showing any outward emotion, but she had solemnly bowed her head as if in prayer. "My father mentioned the Corsicans when he first spoke of you, he called you 'authentic' and 'unwavering.' I imagine he heard of you at the same time you heard of him and realized you'd one day be of use to him." Valencia looked up at him apologetically, "I wish I could tell you more about it."

Cesar had one more question he wanted to ask "I'm not going to devote my faculties to judging your father for what he has done here, or you for aiding him it…But I will ask one question, not because it's critically important to the matter at hand, or because I must know the answer, but because I would like to know the answer."

This interested her more than his other questions had "Yes?"

"Why this place? The Hotel Geraldine?"

Valencia beamed "Geraldine was my mother's name. She died from the influenza in 1919 and her ashes were scattered on the grounds here. Much of the time I had with both my mother and father was spent here at the hotel. When she died, father bought it and renamed it after her. Inviting Von Strichtenheimer here, to a place named after the woman who was engaged to his brother Siegfried just seemed very…appropriate."

Cesar was quiet for a full minute before standing up from his chair.

"Where are you going?" Valencia Decarli asked him.

"I am going to find and kill Felix von Strichtenheimer. All this intrigue and death for a villain such as him? I will consider this night wasted unless it ends with his corpse."

Chapter 13
Lost Nobility

Cesar and Valencia decided that they should find Galopin before attempting to find Von Strichtenheimer. Valencia thought it seemed the right thing considering that Galopin's sole reason for being here was to kill Von Strichtenheimer. Cesar concurred, as there would be greater security in three than two.

They exited the passageways through Galopin's room at the hotel, on the chance that they would find him there. As they expected, Galopin wasn't there.

"You said that you and had Von Strichtenheimer encountered each other in here?"

"I had been looking for Galopin," Cesar said. "…Just as I am now," he added as an afterthought.

Valencia knelt beside the bed and pulled a case out from underneath it. "The major put his case under the bed when I first showed him to his room. It doesn't appear he's returned at any point during the night."

Cesar moved over to the dresser and found that the photo Pryce had taken of Galopin during the Spanish Civil War set on the table next to the bed.

"Actually, it seems that he has." He picked it up and showed the photo to Valencia. "Pryce took this photo, I found it and then gave it to Galopin. So he's definitely been to his room."

"He's clearly not here now" Valencia said plainly. "One of us should stay, if Galopin left this photo here then he'll probably return for it."

"And what will the other one be doing?" Cesar asked suspiciously, sensing Valencia was on the verge of another disappearing act.

"I will search for him downstairs. It will be quicker if I go alone."

"Is it really wise for you to go wandering around by yourself? With Von Strichtenheimer on the loose and intent on killing you?"

Valencia's expression barely concealed her disdain for this question. "I've done a fair job of avoiding his wrath thus far, haven't I? And have you forgotten that I'm armed?"

Cesar scanned her outfit, wondering where she was keeping her gun "Where is…"

She lifted one side of her split skirt just enough to reveal an ankle holster above the boot on her right foot. Sure enough, her gun was there.

"Ah."

Valencia gave him a strange, knowing look. "And just because Von Strichtenheimer intends to kill me doesn't mean he can or will, I'm not his to kill."

Cesar didn't know what this meant, or how her not being "his to kill" was supposed to stop Von Strichtenheimer from doing so. He didn't ask though, and Valencia left anyway.

Now he was alone again. He sat on the edge of Galopin's bed and took the time to reflect. He thought of all who had died tonight…and how they were the fortunate ones. Another war was coming, and they wouldn't have to live through it.

One of Cesar's stranger qualities was how he envied the dead, there was something regal and transcendent about being dead. You were gone, and after a while all that was left was the memory of you, but Cesar knew had seen enough to know that sometimes memories were more powerful than people.

The sound of the wardrobe opening interrupted Cesar's thought process and made him stand up, he was confronted by the sight of Von Strichtenheimer emerging from the wardrobe and striding towards him. Cesar quickly drew his revolver, but before he was able to do anything with it, Von Strichtenheimer lunged forward with his right arm raised. He realized too late that there was a long and thin baton in Von Strichtenheimer's hand.

With incomprehensible speed, Von Strichtenheimer brought the baton down on Cesar's right hand. He felt a jolt of pain as his hand involuntarily opened. Cesar brought up his left hand and punched Von Strichtenheimer in the face, he would've normally hit with his right hand next, but it was still racked with pain.

Von Strichtenheimer then punched him in the face with his free hand. He then slammed the baton against Cesar's left leg, which put him on the floor. Cesar attempted to grab onto Von Strichtenheimer's leg, but he was stopped by a blow to head with the baton.

Von Strichtenheimer began to repeatedly strike Cesar with his baton, occasionally stopping to kick him. Cesar was unable to fight back and just endured the attack on him. By the time Von Strichtenheimer relented, Cesar was barely clinging to consciousness.

He wanted to fight back, even though he was tempted to relax and wait for death. He heard the sound of the secret passage behind the wardrobe opening. He felt Von Strichtenheimer pick him up by his lower legs and begin to drag him across the bedroom floor. The bedroom floor soon turned to the stone floor of the secret passageway, and then it eventually turned to grass.

Cesar started to fully regain consciousness and was able to look towards the lit-up image of the Hotel Geraldine as he was dragged away from it into the dark woods.

"What…" he struggled to say.

"Quiet you fool," Von Strichtenheimer said, "I'm going to make use of you."

The farther they went into the woods, the darker it got, until the lights of the Hotel were no longer visible. Cesar was sure he was about to be murdered, and there was part of him that was willing to accept it, it had been years since he had any fear of death. But he was not willing to let Von Strichtenheimer continue his killing spree.

He wondered in vain if he would have another opportunity to defend himself against Von Strichtenheimer. Could he perhaps grab a rock or piece of forest wood to attack him with? Or maybe he'd be able to get the man's baton and use that? It seemed to be an effective weapon.

The situation was dismal, but Cesar would not give up. If he were to die, then he'd die fighting: This was a promise he made to himself and others long ago.

"What are you doing?" said an unknown voice.

Cesar was struck with confusion and excitement by the sound of this new unrecognizable voice. Whose voice was this? Had someone come to his rescue? What were the odds that they would encounter someone else in the woods at this early hour?

"Help me pick this man up" Von Strichtenheimer said.

"But why have you brought him here?" the unknown person said.

"Don't ask questions."

Cesar's excitement faded, this was an accomplice. Von Strichtenheimer and the other man picked him up by his arms and dragged him forward, Cesar lifted his head and saw that they were approaching a small building made of wood.

One of them kicked the door open to the building and dragged Cesar inside of it, it was dimly lit and smelled less welcoming than the Hotel Geraldine. Cesar was able to make out an assortment of gardening tools that were leaning up against the wall. He just then remembered something that Christophe had told Valencia about the hotel having a groundskeeper. This must've been his shed then, but where was the groundskeeper? Had Von

Strichtenheimer and this unknown accomplice killed him as well?

He was thrown heavily on the ground.

"Get some rope" Von Strichtenheimer ordered.

Cesar gently rolled over onto his side, this allowed him to look at the accomplice as they walked towards a work bench. The shed had enough light so that Cesar was able to see what this new individual looked like, he wore dirty-looking work clothes and he had a flat cap on their head.

When the accomplice came back from the bench with a bundle of rope, Cesar saw that he was a burly, middle-aged man with a large head and a thick grayish-brown beard. As Von Strichtenheimer tied Cesar to one of the support beams, the accomplice looked at him directly. He had dark, uncaring eyes and a hardened face which told a sad story.

Once Von Strichtenheimer finished bounding Cesar to the support beam, he walked around to the groundskeeper with a small brown package in his hand.

"The other portion of your payment" Von Strichtenheimer said, handing the package to his accomplice.

"What must I do now?" the accomplice asked, his voice was mild for a large man like him.

"Go from this place, your previous employers will soon be no more."

Previous employers, Cesar thought. Is this the groundskeeper?

The man-who-was-possibly-the-groundskeeper looked like he was possibly debating if he should express gratitude "Yes...I-"

"I told you to go!" Von Strichtenheimer snapped.

The man took an involuntary step backwards, remained standing there for a few seconds, and then turned to leave the shed. The door shut behind him. Now Cesar was alone with a man who had killed numerous people, including four just this past night.

Cesar immediately began talking "I know why you're doing this. I know what happened."

Von Strichtenheimer looked down at him with scorn "What do you know?"

"I know about what happened with Valencia's mother, about what her father did, the Peithners and what they did, what happened to your family afterwards."

Von Strichtenheimer sneered at him "And who told you these things? Valencia? That child born out of wedlock? Did she also tell you that by the time I was fifteen, I had already attended the funerals of two brothers and five cousins!? That my father's last words were 'I want to go. I want to see them again!?' That my mother rarely even talks anymore?"

"She told me enough...I will not pretend to know anything about what you went through, but I will tell you that I too have-"

Von Strichtenheimer cut him off with a kick to the face. "I am not interested in any futile attempt to equate the two of us" he said harshly. "I will do what I came here to do, and your words will not stop me, any more than they will stop the sun from rising."

Cesar settled on a new tactic, and that was to keep Von Strichtenheimer talking. "Please, just answer me this: Why are you still here? You got what you wanted, you killed Decarli."

"I killed one of the Decarlis."

"You want to kill Valencia too?"

"More then I wanted to kill him."

"Why is that?"

"He was filth that had to be killed, I've killed many like him. But her? I will kill her because of what she represents."

Cesar was confused "What does she represent?"

"She's a mongrel of course, born out of wedlock from a cursed union. Her mother came from a distinguished family and upbringing, and her father was a classless, conniving pig that crawled his way out of the gutter and should've stayed there."

Cesar blinked, and allowed himself two moments to think "That specific part bothers you, does it? Not just that your brother's engagement was ruined, and that your family suffered for it, but that his fiancé was in love with someone beneath her status?"

Von Strichtenheimer looked intensely at him "Do you not see that the two things are related? Do you not see what is happening?"

Cesar just stared at him.

"Europe is dying, entire empires have been destroyed, and the ones that remain are in crisis. Chivalry, tradition, righteousness, societies of structure and limitation: These are things that're slowly vanishing, and one day they will be gone."

He paused for Cesar to say something, but when Cesar said nothing, he continued.

"The age of nobility is ending, and now we are on the verge of an age of peasantry. In Russia, the Tsar and his wife and children are murdered by bandits who call themselves revolutionaries, and now the entire land lives in a fear of Stalin, a serf from Georgia of all places! In Germany the Kaiser abdicates, fifteen years leader Hitler and his Nazi Party take control. Hitler was born an Austrian commoner! He should be less significant than me as an Austrian of birth, but in this world gone insane he's the leader of Germany."

"Do I need to continue? In Italy, Victor Emmanuel must cater to that oaf Mussolini, and Mussolini empowers cretins like Pietro Biassiano. In Spain, they do away with the monarchy in the favor of a leftist Republic, and it only takes a few years for the country to collapse in civil war. And what about your Mexico? Porfirio Diaz leaves and it's ten years of war!"

Cesar had remained quiet until Von Strichtenheimer brought up the Mexican Revolution, an event which he had been present for, which he had experienced and felt, which was part of his identity and influenced every decision he had made over the past twenty years. And now this lunatic was going to offhandedly mention it to him while he was tied up in a shed?

"Do not speak of things you don't understand!" Cesar yelled, not bothering to hide his anger.

He had expected Von Strichtenheimer to kick him again, but instead the man just seemed to become more histrionic. "The world is breaking down! Values of kingliness and nobility have been discarded, and now power is the hands of people who don't know how to use it! Entire nations are being run by the sons of shoemakers, blacksmiths, and clerks! And yet we're surprised that the world is once again on the brink of war!?"

Cesar barely knew what to say. He was astounded by the pompousness and certitude of this disenfranchised nobleman, how he had self-servingly correlated the decline of Europe's noble classes with the world's presently volatile geopolitical situation. He was like a Roman Emperor without an empire to command, and thus could only lash out at a world that had left him behind.

"Do you not have anything to say!?" Von Strichtenheimer shouted.

"I don't need to say anything…" Cesar said, sounding bored "… Because you've made it clear that you have such insight and awareness into the ills of the world, and therefore you are justified in any vile act you wish to partake in."

"Enough of this" Von Strichtenheimer declared. "I will not waste my time arguing with you. Tell me where Valencia Decarli is."

"She went looking for Galopin."

"Who she and her father intended to kill me" he said triumphantly, as if he should receive praise for realizing this. "You and I will go back to the Hotel. You will take me to her, and then I will kill her. In exchange, I'll let you live, just like I let live that man who just left."

"I'd rather you kill me," Cesar said seriously.

"You'd give up your life to protect her!?" Von Strichtenheimer said in amazement.

"I'd give up my life to protect my nobility," Cesar said sleekly.

Von Strichtenheimer's eyes widened as he realized he was being made fun of. They then narrowed as he looked down on Cesar with piercing contempt.

"Then you and I will wait here. She will come looking for you, and when she does, you'll watch me kill her. Once I've finished, I will kill you as well."

"And this will accomplish what in your mind? Will it reverse the crisis of nobility that you perceive to be happening?"

"I do not do this to prevent the coming age of peasanty" Von Strichtenheimer said quickly, a disgruntled look on his face. "I do this because I am not a peasant. So long as there is breath in me, I will not abide by a world made by my lessers. Even in an age of lambs, I will always be a lion."

"You do it because you must" said a familiar female voice.

Both men looked to see Valencia Decarli standing in the open door of the shed. Felix von Strichtenheimer stared at her with eyes of pure hatred. Valencia on the other hand regarded him with look of resolute confidence.

Cesar could only look on disbelievingly as the two of them stared each other down.

Chapter 14
Darkness and Light

Valencia Decarli did not have the appearance of someone who was afraid to face down a man who had murdered dozens of people, including her own father, and who was hellbent on killing her as well. Cesar was not typically a fearful person, but even he couldn't comprehend the composure and lack of fear she displayed.

Von Strichtenheimer broke into a deranged smile "You…" he mumbled through his teeth "That you would…"

"Yes?" Valencia said softy, as if she were speaking to a shy child.

"That you would even show yourself to me!" Von Strichtenheimer eventually blurted out in a loud, outraged voice. His demented smile gone "That you would not hide like the vermin that you are! Instead you seek me out and prove that you have no shame for what you are and what has been done to me! I, whose family was destroyed by the insolence and corruption of your criminal father! I, who've sworn that there will be justice for these crimes!"

Valencia patiently listened to him, her hands crossed in front of her. When he stopped to catch his breath, she spoke. "Do you not realize that my father did not intend for the events of 1913 to play out as they did?" she asked, speaking in clear, controlled voice. "He never wanted anyone to die, or for the Peithners to go as far as they did. He simply wanted to be with my mother-"

"I do not care!" Von Strichtenheimer roared. "He was an outsider and an interloper, and it was he who caused a crisis that brought the downfall of a venerable family. All for a woman he had no right to, a woman of noble blood who he debased when he bore you!"

"He loved her" Valencia said simply.

"Then this is the price he pays!"

"He already paid it when you killed him."

His demented smile returned to his face "Oh no, that was only the first payment. The second payment is you."

"Yes, yes. We suspected as much. You wish to kill me as well" Valencia said, as if she was having a mundane conversation.

"I do not wish for anything! I will kill you, I will enjoy killing you more than I did your father, more than I have enjoyed killing anyone."

Valencia raised an eyebrow "I'm that awful?"

"You are an abomination. The bastard child of a whore and a degenerate criminal."

"Well kill me if you must, but please let Cesar go, he hasn't done anything to you."

"I will make you watch while I burn him alive if I so please!" he shrieked, looking agitated.

"Burn him alive?" Valencia said with interest. "Oh fascinating, is that how I will die?"

Von Strichtenheimer immediately calmed down "I haven't decided how I will kill you," he said in a considerate tone. "A quick death would be far too merciful, a slow death too glorious. Should I make it so that you disappear completely? Or would it be preferable if someone found your broken lifeless body? And what condition would you be in? Disfigured beyond recognition? Perhaps I would rather that whoever finds you knows that it's you."

"I am flattered that so much thought was put into this."

"I spent months thinking about how I would kill your father. I chose poison because it's used to kill vermin, which was ultimately what he was…Unfortunately, I could not make up my mind on how to kill you."

He looked around at the various tools and landscaping implements on the wall. "But I have plenty to choose from…"

Cesar just stared at the bizarre interaction that was taking place, wondering how it could possibly end in any way that was beneficial to himself or to Valencia.

"I would like to know something before you begin" Valencia said casually, still showing no indication that she was on the verge of being murdered.

"And what's that?"

"The woman in Strasbourg."

"What woman in-" A look of recognition soon swept over Von Strichtenheimer's face. He smiled wolfishly. "Ah yes, I know what you're talking about."

"Did you know she was my mother's aunt?" Valencia said, frowning.

"No, only that she mattered to your mother. I was in France looking for information on your mother. I met a man who had been a servant for one of your mother's parents, he told me about an old woman that knew your mother. I went to Strasbourg with the intention of simply having a conversation with her, but…" He chuckled cruelly. "I don't think she liked me very much."

Von Strichtenheimer laughed more.

Valencia shed her usual composedness and glared daggers at the laughing murderer before her. In her eyes alone, she conveyed a hatred that rivaled that of Von Strichtenheimer.

"Anyway…" Von Strichtenheimer said once he finished laughing, "In the old woman's bedroom, I found a strongbox that was filled with letters from your mother. They were incredibly valuable, I got your father's name from them, and your name as well."

"My mother sent letters to her?" a surprised Valencia asked, this was news to her

"Your father wouldn't have approved if he knew?"

She placed the side of her hand on her face, her expression sentimental "That does sound like something she would've done."

"If only she had been as smart as him?"

Cesar saw something in the shadows behind Von Strichtenheimer that almost made him scream. A pale face was barely visible in the dark. For a moment, Cesar wondered if he was seeing a ghost…but then he recognized who's face it was.

Dieudonne Galopin took a quiet step forward, allowing Cesar to see him more clearly.

Valencia looked over at Cesar and communicated to him with her eyes. She knew that he had saw Galopin, she knew that Cesar saw her looking at him, and now she was expecting something from him.

Von Strichtenheimer noticed Valencia looking at Cesar and looked over himself as if expecting to see Cesar loose from his binds. He turned his attention back to Valencia,

"Why -"

"Look at me!" Cesar shouted at the top of his lungs.

Von Strichtenheimer jerked his head towards Cesar, glaring down at him with a shock that quickly turned to suspicion.

Galopin took this as his opportunity to emerge from the shadows, a trench knife in his right-hand. Von Strichtenheimer spun around to see the man coming towards him. Galopin acted, grabbing his target's shoulder with one hand and using the other to drive the dagger into his stomach.

Von Strichtenheimer made a sound that could be described as a whimper. Galopin pulled the knife out his stomach, and he fell to the ground.

"Very good Major," Valencia remarked gracefully. "And you as well Cesar."

"Could you please untie me?" Cesar asked disconcertedly, still adjusting to what had happened.

Valencia undid Cesar's binds and helped him to his feet. Galopin retrieved Cesar's LeMat Revolver from Von Strichtenheimer's person. "I think you've shown that I can trust you with this Monsieur Mondragon," He tossed it to him.

Cesar looked at the only door to the shed "Major, how did you get in here?"

"Through a tunnel, there's a trap door under that rug."

Von Strichtenheimer stirred from where he lay on the ground.

"He's not dead yet?" Cesar asked pitifully, looking at Von Strichtenheimer the same way he'd look at a dying animal.

"He will be soon enough" Galopin said, sounding pleased. "It's just a question of how soon you'd like it to be."

"You insinuate that I'm a sadist?" Valencia remarked coldly. "End his terrible existence and be done with it."

As Von Strichtenheimer lay on the ground, he extended his right arm out and raised it towards Galopin, almost as if he was reaching out for him. The French army officer stared at him furiously "You ask for mercy? Did you give Pryce mercy? Or all those you killed in Spain? Do you–"

Within a second, a small pistol appeared in Von Strichtenheimer's hand.

Cesar opened his voice to shout, but he was too late.

A shot rang out. Galopin's hand went up to his neck as blood began to pour from it.

Valencia grabbed Cesar's revolver and shot Von Strichtenheimer in his chest. He fell still.

Galopin lumbered forward, with his hand out towards Cesar and Valencia. They both were able to catch him before he fell to the ground.

"We must get him to the hotel" Valencia said urgently.

"Grab one of his arms" Cesar commanded.

Cesar and Valencia, with one of Galopin's arms over each of their shoulders, made their way out of the shed.

Having been beaten into near unconsciousness and dragged into the woods, Cesar had no idea as to what direction the Hotel Geraldine was in. Valencia did though and was able to guide them through the woods as they carried Galopin. The morning sun had started to rise, which made the ground in front of them easier to see.

Galopin kept his head tilted in a sloppy attempt to slow the loss of blood from his neck, but it still trickled down his chin and onto his clothes.

"It's no use!" Cesar said with a growl "He's going to bleed out."

"We have to try and save him" Valencia asserted. "I owe him that much after what my father and I put him through."

"I hear him!" Galopin groaned frantically.

"What did you say?" Cesar asked sharply.

"He's here!"

Cesar and Valencia looked at each other as if accusing the other of knowing what Galopin was talking about, but then they heard footfalls on grass behind them. The two of them looked around and were surprised to see Von Strichtenheimer slouching towards them. Despite having been stabbed and then shot, he had found enough strength to climb to his feet and give chase. He was walking stiff-legged, each step looked painful. His pants and the ground beneath him were spattered with the blood from his open chest wounds. His right arm hung limply out in front of him, his hand still clutching the sleeve-gun.

There was no longer any hatred on his face, instead he wore a haggard mask of determination. Before he died, he would kill more.

Cesar drew his revolver, took care aim, and shot Von Strichtenheimer just above the heart.

Von Strichtenheimer stopped in his tracks as he was shot a second time. He glanced down at the wounds in his chest as if he had only just realized he had them. Blood began to appear at his lips. He attempted to keep moving forward, but instead fell to the ground. Cesar shot him once more for good measure. Felix Von Strichtenheimer would not be standing up again.

Without commenting about what happened, Valencia urged them to continue towards the hotel. "We must keep moving Cesar!"

It did not take them long to find their way out of the woods. Once they were back at the Hotel Geraldine, it took them far longer to find a door inside and spent the next minute or so walking along the outside walls. They eventually arrived at a small door that looked like an entrance for servants.

They entered through the door and Cesar was surprised to see they were in the kitchen, but it was empty, suggesting the kitchen staff were long gone by now. The blood of the two men who had been killed earlier that morning was also nowhere in sight, having been wiped clean perhaps immediately after it happened

Valencia led them through the kitchen to the same dining room where they had eaten dinner. In the past several hours, five of the ten dinner guests had died. Together Cesar and Valencia heaved Galopin onto the table, so he was lying flat on his back.

"I will find Doctor Gounelle! Please stay with him!" She ran out into the hall before Cesar could say another word.

Cesar looked towards Galopin, who was staring at the ceiling with a distant look.

"Major?" Cesar said.

Galopin's eyes began to flutter, Cesar grabbed him by the shoulders and shook him briefly "Major, you need to not close your eyes or fall asleep! You need to stay with me until help arrives!"

"It is no use" Galopin said drowsily. "My name has been written in the book. I survived the Western Front, survived the Rif, survived fighting the Falangists in Spain; but it was one man with a sleeve-gun that managed to kill me.

"The doctor is coming" Cesar said, trying to hide his lack of hope for Galopin's survival. "You just need to wait a few minutes longer."

"No!" Galopin said, suddenly speaking loudly. "This is my penance, it is proof that I am a fool for coming here!"

Cesar felt annoyed. "You should've told Decarli no," he said harshly.

"Heh, it is not about Decarli" Galopin croaked proudly. "I wanted to kill Von Strichtenheimer. Good people died by his hand in Spain. The war has been over for months, but a part of me did not want to stop fighting it. I did not want to accept that the Republican cause was lost, and that another great nation had fallen under the unworthy rule of an overdressed autocrat."

"I settled for killing one more fascist," He laughed painfully. "And now I've done that, with the help of Mademoiselle Decarli of course."

"Only now Pryce is dead," Cesar pointed out, "And it seems certain you will be as well. Was killing Von Strichtenheimer worth both your lives?"

"No…" Galopin said quietly, "Pryce and I could have died killing fifty fascists and it would've made no difference. The world is still as it is, and war is coming. *Ce putain de connard Hitler…*"

Cesar spoke enough French to know this meant "That fucking asshole Hitler."

"He wants retribution for Versailles, he will attack France, and now I will not be there for it. I have thrown my remaining time away in pursuit of personal vengeance and abandoned my fellow countrymen and women."

Cesar grew aggravated with Galopin's melodrama and self-pity, he grabbed the dying man by the head and looked him in the eyes "I will be there for them!" Cesar insisted "I will be there along with countless others. France is not yours to protect, its burden is no longer yours. The burden is on all who remain and all who will soon be, it is our duty to prove that we are worthy of the past.

You are about to become part of that past, have some dignity and die quietly."

The two men held each other's stare for many long moments.

"You are worthy of your first name" Galopin said finally.

Cesar was sure this was a compliment, but he wasn't certain what it meant.

"He is here" Galopin said.

"What?

Galopin was dead, Cesar made a gentle noise, and closed the French officer's eyes.

The dining room door opened, Cesar turned to see Doctor Gounelle appear.

"Where is Valencia?" Cesar asked the doctor.

The doctor looked bemused "She told me you would be waiting for me here."

Before the doctor had finished his sentence, Cesar was hit with the understanding that he would likely not see Valencia Decarli anymore tonight.

"You're too late, Galopin is dead" Cesar said bluntly.

Doctor Gounelle peered down at the French officer's dead body "So much death tonight," he lamented, "Would you believe me if I told you that there have been times where I've seen greater death than this?"

Cesar thought of all the death he had seen, "Yes, I would." He left the dining room without saying anything else to Gounelle.

He went on to search the drawing room for Valencia, and the apartment she shared with her father, and the basement where she and her father had planned the night's events. The Hotel Geraldine was plenty big enough for Valencia to hide in, but Cesar knew that she was long gone.

Alexander Decarli had been successful in what he set out to do: His daughter was alive, and the man who wished to kill her was dead. It had come at the cost of his own life, but it seemed that such a loss was acceptable to him. His daughter, who had been the most important thing to him, was free to live the rest of her life as she saw fit.

There was nothing left for Cesar to do, it was time for him to go. But before he did, there was one other person he wanted to speak to.

Cesar went to Rombauer's bedroom. It was hard to miss with the bullet holes in the door and Turina's dead body against the wall opposite it. He briefly glanced at the dead body as he knocked on the door.

"Mister Dickerson?"

"Mondragon?"

"Can you let me in sir?"

"Uh…yes. If you'll be so kind to wait as I remove the barricade."

It took a minute for Dickerson to move enough furniture to open the door and let Cesar in. Nearly everything in the room had been used to block the door from intruders, save for two chairs, a small table and the armoire that led to the passageways.

Cesar looked around the room "Where's Rombauer?"

"He's asleep in the bathroom."

He went to look, sure enough the engineer was sound asleep in the empty bathtub.

He returned to Dickerson, whose suit jacket and tie lay folded on the bed. The American stood there in his dress shirt, pants, and shoes; his hands in his pocket as he silently waited for the latest news of the night.

"It's all over sir," Cesar said, loving the taste of these words. "There's no more danger, and I have the answers I've been looking for. If you so choose, I can enlighten you on what's happened tonight."

Dickerson smiled gladly at this good news and gestured towards the two chairs "Shall we?"

Cesar did most of the talking. Dickerson's gladness was soon replaced by amazement "Decarli did all this just to get Von Strichtenheimer?"

"I saw his psychosis for myself, he was someone who needed to be expunged. I don't know if this was the way to go about it. Though it seems an ordeal to try and understand what went on in the late Alexander's mind."

"And where's Miss Decarli?"

"I think she's gone."

"Gone where?"

"She's gone" Cesar repeated.

Dickerson understood. "Just the three of us then?"

"So it seems," he said brusquely. He glanced over at the bathroom where Rombauer was "And what of him?"

"Ah…In the time you were gone, I had a conversation with the Doctor. He has not yet agreed to provide his services to the western powers. But now that he's aware that the opposing powers are after him, he'll be relocating from his residence in Gothenburg. My handlers will be pleased to hear this."

"Everything is as it should be then," Cesar said gladly. The adrenaline of the night was wearing off and he felt his body craving food and sleep. "I really should be leaving Mister Dickerson, I advise you and Rohrbach to do the same."

"Before you go, I'd like just a few minutes of your time."

Cesar felt himself physically protest the notion of remaining at the hotel any longer. But he couldn't deny he was curious about what Dickerson wanted.

"If you give me one of your cigarettes, I'll talk as long as you want."

"Do you smoke?"

"No."

Dickerson didn't question this and shared a cigarette with Cesar. They talked idly for a minute before the conversation shifted to the matter Dickerson was interested in.

"I am familiar with the work you've done as an investigator. Have you ever considered working for American intelligence?"

Cesar was weary of this question "That depends on what that work entails. I have no interest in working for the United Fruit Company."

Dickerson seemed appalled by the very suggestion of it "Those banana-brained idiots? Good Lord no, you'd be doing actual work. You do realize a war is coming right?"

"With the Nazis?"

"And their co-belligerent states."

"How certain are you of this?"

"Very. Today is August 4, the Germans and Soviets are putting the finish touches on a non-aggression pact. It's been conducted in secret, but it should be announced before the end of this month."

"I thought the Nazis hated the Soviet Union?"

"They do, but they have long term objectives. This wouldn't be happening unless the Germans had plans for military action. It could be they want to attack the west and ensure that the east remains docile, but it may also be the case that a non-aggression pact with the Soviets is to prepare for military action in the east. My gut feeling is that Poland is in trouble: They're the only state in the region that has the poor unfortunate luck of sharing a land border with both Hitler and Stalin.

"Britain and France wouldn't allow that" Cesar suggested.

Dickerson scoffed "They're likely to declare war if that's what you mean, but your guess is as good as mine what they'll do once they've done that.

"And the west will need me for this war?"

"The west will need all the competent people it can muster, if not more than that. Right now, we have less than that."

"Why should I help you?"

Dickerson raised his eyebrow and crossed his arms, apparently taking issue with having been asked this question "Do you not think the Allied cause is worthy?"

"I think what's occurring in Germany and Italy will end badly, it's only a question of how badly. But this does not mean I trust in the benevolence of the western powers."

Dickerson smirked "Smart man, but don't think of it as placing trust in the western powers. Instead think of it as the opportunity to be a detriment to the Nazis and all that they stand for."

Cesar put out the cigarette "Again, it depends on what the work entails. So be specific about what you have in mind."

"You'd be gathering intelligence, talking to people we need on our side and not theirs. If the war gets bad, and I foresee that it will, you'd be doing sabotage, professional thievery, assassination."

Cesar regarded Dickerson dubiously. "You wouldn't be asking me unless you knew that I've done those things before."

"Before I came here, I ascertained the proper details on all the names on the invitation; yours stuck out to me. You may be surprised to find that your name still elicits a reaction to certain people in the United States and Mexico."

Cesar stared hard at him. It appeared that Dickerson knew more of his past than Decarli and his daughter did.

Dickerson was near capable of reading his mind and made the effort to assure him that his past actions and affairs had no bearing on the present offer.

"Don't overthink it son. We know who you are, we know what you've done, we want to use you."

Cesar tried to reason, but his brain felt debilitated after everything that happened tonight "Contact me as soon as this war of yours starts, and we'll talk about what you need done. Right now, I must find a place to sleep."

"This hotel is not sufficient?"

"I never want to see this hotel again for as long as I live."

Cesar left the staffroom and immediately went up to his

bedroom on the second floor. His packed suitcase was the same place it was when he last came to this room many hours ago. That made things simpler, all he had to do was grab it and leave, but that was before he saw that a note had been left on it. Dreading what may be written on it, Cesar picked it up.

Dear Cesar Mondragon

If you're reading this note, it means that I have left the Geraldine. Ordinarily, I think it's amiss to make such a sudden departure, but given the most unordinary nature of this event, I trust that you will forgive me.

The Grand Ducal Gendarmerie has been alerted and will be arriving sometime this morning. My father made one of his arrangements with them. They had a limited awareness of what was occurring tonight and understood they were not to interlope until they were called. I imagine they will see to the bodies that have been left here and speak to the hotel staff, who have been instructed to cooperate with them. If my advice is of any value to you, then you should leave before their arrival. No one will pursue you, although I cannot promise that you won't be recognized if you ever return to Luxembourg.

I apologize for the circumstances under which my father and I led you to the Geraldine. If you find my apology lacking (and I most certainly would if I were in your position) then I suggest that it would be in your interest to travel to Zurich. I suggest this because if you were to go to the Credit Suisse bank in that city and tell them your name, there would be an account there with generous amounts of currency in it. My father set this money aside for you. He had great faith that you would play the role we hoped you would play.

Please do not try to find me. I will not be found unless I wish to be found, it's one of the many crafts I learned from my father. If it's meant that we are to meet again, then hopefully it will be

under more pleasant circumstances.
    Thank you for the service you provided.
Valencia Decarli

Cesar sighed, it seemed there was something to be gained from this night after all. He felt his animosity towards Alexander and his daughter lighten. They were both utterly Machiavellian and delighted in using people, but they were obviously not without their standards and principles. Had Galopin and Pryce survived the night, he was sure they would've been rewarded as well.

The final thought he had on the manner was the prospect of meeting Valencia again. The idea both frightened and amused him.

He took Valenca's note with him as he left the room and locked the door. When he went downstairs to the lobby, he saw that the concierge named Nicholas was still there. While people were losing their lives, and old scores were being settled, this man had apparently never once left his post.

He went up to Nicholas to return his key. Just as when he first arrived, the man seemed intent on not looking at Cesar. Annoyed, he noisily dropped the key on the front desk. Nicholas peered at the key, and then looked up at Cesar, his eyebrow arched.

"Do you have the slightest notion of what's gone on here tonight?" Cesar asked him flatly.

Nicholas didn't say anything at first and just stared for a few seconds. He then chuckled softly and gave a knowing look. "Nothing that hasn't happened here before."

It took Cesar several moments to realize what this meant. Once he fully understood, he began to think of all the previous "formal gatherings" the Decarlis' had had in this hotel. Surely this wasn't the first time they used this hotel for their own devices? Had there been other murders? What the hell else had occurred in this demented shithouse of theirs?

He felt something that resembled nausea and took it as his cue to make a beeline for the hotel's front doors.

He would drive back to Gutland and return the Mercedes-G5 Benz he had rented. He would then cross the international border and search for an inn or a hotel in the nearest town. He would eat something and get whatever sleep he could.

When he woke, he would begin on his trails back to England. The money he had waiting in Switzerland would remain where it was for the time being.

Howard Curtin IV has lived in Arizona all his life. As a teenager, Howard realized he wanted to write stories and began a journey that he's still on. He graduated from the University of Arizona with a Bachelor of Arts in English. Howard is a student of history, philosophy, and all that is weird and wonderful. But his greatest passion is fiction.